Mrs. Hannah Cowley, Hannah Cowley

A Bold Stroke for a Husband

A comedy, as acted at the Theatre Royal, in Covent Garden

Mrs. Hannah Cowley, Hannah Cowley

A Bold Stroke for a Husband
A comedy, as acted at the Theatre Royal, in Covent Garden

ISBN/EAN: 9783337251949

Printed in Europe, USA, Canada, Australia, Japan

Cover: Foto ©Andreas Hilbeck / pixelio.de

More available books at **www.hansebooks.com**

A Bold Stroke for a Hufband,

A

COMEDY,

AS ACTED AT THE

THEATRE ROYAL,

IN

COVENT GARDEN.

By Mrs. COWLEY.

THIRD EDITION.

LONDON:

PRINTED BY M. SCOTT, CHANCERY-LANE, FOR

T. EVANS, PATERNOSTER-ROW.

MDCCLXXXIV.

PROLOGUE.

NOW, by my fanguine hopes, our author cries,
 With expectation fparkling in her eyes,
There's nothing here fhould fcare me that I fee,
They all are faplings of the tough old tree :
Women, who wear Elyfium in their look,
And men, unconquer'd as their native oak.
But yet a word or two I'll briefly fay,
To prove we're right in naming of our play.

 Of human conduct, in each varied fcene,
Th' extreme fucceeds beyond the patient mean ;
If eminence in rank our bofoms fire,
If merit to preferment dare afpire,
Follow the active, not the formal part,
" And fnatch a grace beyond the rules of art."

         Bold

Bold Strokes, from bounding genius firmly ftruck,
Attract fuccefs, more than the turns of luck.
The bankrupt fwindler, though to pay unable,
Oft mends his fortune by the E O table ;
Or, failing there, he acts a braver part,
And takes a purfe,—*a Bold Stroke for the cart.*
The gamefter too forgets each tender tie,
And ventures his laft guinea on a die,
'Till ruin'd, and repenting of the evil,
He hangs himfelf—*a Bold Stroke for the Devil.*
The fortune hunter fports a fuit of lace,
In this a Count, a Lord in t'other place,
Succefs at length, begins his married life
At Gretna Green—*a Bold Stroke for a Wife.*

But are bold ftrokes to vicious men confin'd ?
Does virtue lie inactive in the mind ?
It cannot be, while England's genius breathes,
And many a brow is deck'd with laurel wreaths.
Bold ftrokes in war are England's greateft pride ;
Think how a Hood has liv'd, a Manners died

Our play holds forth the conqueft of a heart,
By one bold ftroke of nature, not of art.
A female pen calls female virtue forth,
And fairly fhews to man her fex's worth.
Could men but fee what female fenfe can do,
How apt their wit, their conftancy—how true ;

In vain would rakes the married ſtate revile,
Nor with the wanton, precious time beguile.
   Such is our aim, to rectify the age,
By bringing riſing follies on the ſtage ;
Be then propitious, let our fears decreaſe,
While you, with plaudits, ratify the peace!

DRAMATIS PERSONÆ.

DON JULIO,	Mr. *LEWIS.*
DON CARLOS,	Mr. *WROUGHTON.*
DON CÆSAR,	Mr. *QUICK.*
DON VINCENTIO,	Mr. *EDWIN.*
DON GARCIA,	Mr. *WHITFIELD.*
VASQUEZ,	Mr. *FEARON.*
GASPER,	Mr. *WILSON.*
PEDRO,	Mr. *STEVENS.*

OLIVIA,	Mrs. *MATTOCKS.*
VICTORIA,	Mrs. *ROBINSON.*
LAURA,	Mrs. *WHITFIELD.*
MARCELLA,	Miss *MORRIS.*
MINETTE,	Mrs. *WILSON.*
INIS,	Miss *PLATT.*
SANCHA,	Mrs. *DAVENETT.*

SCENE, *SPAIN.*

A Bold Stroke for a Huſband.

ACT I. SCENE I.

A Street in Madrid.

Enter SANCHA *from a Houſe, ſhe advances, then runs back, and beckons to* PEDRO *within.*

SANCHA.

HIST! Pedro! Pedro!

Enter PEDRO.

There he is : do'ſt ſee him? juſt turning by St. Antony in the corner. Now, do you tell him that your miſtreſs is not at home; and if his jealous Donſhip ſhould inſiſt on ſearching the houſe, as he did yeſterday, ſay that ſomebody is ill—the black has got a fever, or that——

PED. Pho, pho, get you in. Don't I know that the duty of a lacquey in Madrid is to lie with a good grace? I have been ſtudying it now for a whole week, and I'll defy Don or Devil to ſurprize me into a truth. Get you in, I ſay—here he comes. [*Exit.* SANCHA.

Enter CARLOS.

[PEDRO *ſtruts up to him*] Donna Laura is not at home, Sir.

B   CAR.

CAR. Not at home!—come, Sir, what have you received for telling that lie?

PED. Lie!—Lie!—Signor!—

CAR. It muſt be a lie by your promptneſs in delivering it.——What a fool does your miſtreſs truſt!—A clever raſcal would have waited my approach, and, delivering the meſſage with eaſy coolneſs, deceived me——*thou* haſt been on the watch, and runneſt towards me with a face of ſtupid importance, bawling, that ſhe may hear through the lettice how well thou obeyeſt her,—" *Donna Laura is not at home, Sir.*"

PED. Hear through the lettice—hah! by'r lady ſhe muſt have long ears, to reach from the grotto in the garden to the ſtreet.

CAR. Hah! [*ſeizes him*] Now, Sir, your ears ſhall be longer, if you do not tell me who is with her in the grotto.

PED. In the grotto, Sir!——did I ſay any thing about the grotto? I——I only meant that——

CAR. Fool!—doſt thou trifle with me? who is with her?   [*Pinching his ear.*

PED. Oh!—why nobody, Sir—only the pretty young gentleman's valet, waiting for an anſwer to a letter he brought. There! I have ſaved my ears at the expence of my place. I have worn this fine coat but a week, and I ſhall be ſent back to Segovia for not being able to lie, though I have been learning the art ſix days and nights.

CAR. Well—come this way—if thou wilt promiſe to be faithful to me, I will not betray thee: nor at preſent enter the houſe.

PED. Oh, Sir, bleſſings on you!

CAR. How often does the pretty young gentleman viſit her?

PED.

PED. Every day, Sir—If he miſſes, madam's ſtark wild.

CAR. Where does he live?

PED. Truly, I know not, Sir.

CAR. How! [*Menacing.*

PED. By the honeſty of my mother, I cannot tell, Sir. She calls him Florio ;—that's his Chriſtian name—his Heathen name I never heard.

CAR. You muſt acquaint me when they are next together.

PED. Lord, Sir, if there ſhould be any blood ſpilt!

CAR. Promiſe,—or I'll lead thee by the ears to the grotto.

PED. I promiſe, I promiſe.

CAR. There, take that, [*gives money*] and if thou art faithful I'll treble it. Now go in, and be a good lad— and, d'ye hear?—you may tell lies to every body elſe, but remember you muſt always ſpeak truth to me.

PED. I will, Sir,—I will. [*Exit, looking at the money.*

CAR. 'Tis well my paſſion is extinguiſhed, for I can now act with coolneſs ; I'll wait patiently for the hour of their ſecurity, and take them in the ſofteſt moments of their love. But if ever I truſt to woman more—may every——

Enter two women, veiled, followed by JULIO.

JULIO. Fye, ladies! keep your curtains drawn ſo late! The ſun is up—'tis time to look abroad—[*tries to remove their veils*] Nay, if you are determined on night and ſilence, I take my leave. A woman without prattle, is like Burgundy without ſpirit.—Bright eyes, to touch me, :muſt belong to ſweet tongues. [*Going.*

CAR. Sure 'tis Julio. Hey!

JULIO.

JULIO. [*Returning*] Don Carlos ? Yes, by all the fober gods of matrimony !—Why, what bufinefs, goodman gravity, can'ft thou have in Madrid—I underftand you are *married*—quietly fettled in your own paftures—father of a family, and the inftructive companion of country vine dreffers——ha ! ha !

CAR. 'Tis falfe, by heaven !—I have forfworn the country—left my family, and run away from my wife.

JULIO. Really ! then matrimony has not totally deftroyed thy free will.

CAR. 'Tis with difficulty I have preferv'd it though ; for women, thou knoweft, are moft unreafonable beings ! as foon as I had exhaufted my ftock of love tales, which, with management, lafted beyond the honey-moon, madam grew fullen,—I found home dull, and amufed myfelf with the pretty peafants of the neighbourhood——Worfe and worfe !—we had nothing now but faintings, tears and hyfterics for twenty-four honey-moons more.—So one morning I gave her in her fleep a farewell kifs, to comfort her when fhe fhould awake, and pofted to Madrid ; where, if it was not for the remembrance of the clog at my heel, I fhould bound o'er the regions of pleafure, with more fpirit than a young Arabian on his mountains.

JULIO. Do you find this clog no hindrance in affairs of gallantry ?

CAR. Not much.—In that houfe there—but, d—— her, fhe's perfidious !—in that houfe is a woman of beauty, with pretenfions to character and fortune, who devoted herfelf to my paffion.

JULIO. If fhe's perfidious, give her to the winds.

CAR. Ah, but there *is* a rub, Julio, I have been a fool—a woman's fool !—In a ftate of intoxication, fhe wheedled me, or rather cheated me, out of a fettlement.

JULIO.

JULIO. Pho ! is that——

CAR. Oh ! but you know not its nature. A fettlement of lands that both honour and gratitude ought to have preferved facred from fuch bafe alienation.—In fhort, if I cannot recover them, I am a ruined man.

JULIO. Nay, this feems a worfe clog than t'other—Poor Carlos ! fo bewiv'd and be——

CAR. Prithee have compaffion.

Enter a Servant with a letter to Julio, he reads it, and then nods to the Servant, who exits.

CAR. An appointment, I'll be fworn, by that air of myftery and fatisfaction—come, be friendly, and communicate.

JULIO. [*Putting up the letter*] You are married, Carlos ;—that's all I have to fay—you are married.

CAR. Pho, that's paft long ago, and ought to be forgotten ; but if a man does a foolifh thing once, he'll hear of it all his life.

JULIO. Aye, the time has been when thou might'ft have been entrufted with fuch a dear fecret,—when I might have opened the billet, and feafted thee with the fweet meandring ftrokes at the bottom, which form her name, when——

CAR. What, 'tis from a woman then ?

JULIO. It is.

CAR. Handfome ?

JULIO. Hum—not abfolutely handfome, but fhe'll pafs, with one who has not had his tafte fpoilt by—*matrimony.*

CAR. Malicious dog !—Is fhe young ?

JULIO. Under twenty—fair complexion, azure eyes, red lips, teeth of pearl, polifhed neck, fine turn'd fhape, graceful——

CAR.

CAR. Hold, Julio, if thou lov'ft me !—Is it poffible fhe can be fo bewitching a creature ?

JULIO. 'Tis poffible—though, to deal plainly, I never faw her ; but I love my own pleafure fo well, that I could fancy all that, and ten times more.

CAR. What ftar does fhe inhabit ?

JULIO. *Irradiate* thou fhould'ft have faid, after fuch a defcription—but, faith, I know not ; my orders are to be in waiting at feven, at the Prado.

CAR. Prado!—hey!—gad! can't you take me with you? for though I have forfworn the fex myfelf, and have done with them for ever, yet I may be of ufe to *you*, you know.

JULIO. Faith, I can't fee that—however, as you are a poor woe-begone *married* mortal, I'll have compaffion, and fuffer thee to come.

CAR. Then I am a man again ! Wife, avaunt !—mif-trefs, farewell !—At feven you fay ?

JULIO. Exactly.

CAR. I'll meet thee at Philippi ! 　　 [*Exit. feverally.*

S C E N E II.

A fpacious Garden belonging to Don CÆSAR.

Enter MINETTE *and* INIS.

MIN. There, will that do ? My lady fent me to make her up a nofegay ; thefe orange flowers are deli-cious, and this rofe, how fweet !

INIS. Pho, what fignifies wearing fweets in her bofom, unlefs they would fweeten her manners ?—'tis amazing you can be fo much at your eafe ; one might think your lady's tongue was a lute, and her morning fcolds an agreeable ferenade.

MIN.

MIN. So they are—Custom you know. I have been used to her music now these two years, and I don't believe I could relish my breakfast without it.

INIS. I would rather never break my fast, than do it on such terms. What a difference between your mistress and mine; Donna Victoria is as much too gentle, as her cousin is too harsh.

MIN. Aye, and you see what she gets by it; had she been more spirited, perhaps her husband would not have forsaken her;—men enlisted under the matrimonial banner, like those under the King's, would be often tempted to run away from their colours, if fear did not keep them in dread of desertion.

INIS. If making a husband *afraid* is the way to keep him faithful, I believe your lady will be the happiest wife in Spain.

MIN. Ha, ha, ha! how people may be deceived!—nay, how people are deceived!—but time will discover all things.

INIS. What! what is there a secret in the business, Minette? if there is, hang time! let's have it directly.

MIN. Now, if I dar'd but tell ye—lud! lud! how I could surprize ye!—— [*Going.*

INIS. [*Stopping her*] Don't go.

MIN. I must go; I am on the very brink of betraying my mistress,—I must leave you—mercy upon me!—it rises like new bread.

INIS. I hope it will choak ye, if you stir 'till I know all.

MIN. Will you never breathe a syllable?

INIS. Never.

B 4 MIN.

Min. Will you ſtrive to forget it the moment you have heard it ?

Inis. I'll ſwear to myſelf forty times a-day to forget it.

Min. You are ſure you will not let me ſtir from this ſpot till you know the whole.

Inis. Not as far as a thruſh hops.

Min. So ! now, then, in one word,—here it goes. Though every body ſuppoſes my lady an errant ſcold, ſhe's no more a——

Don Cæsar *without.*

Out upon't ! e——h——h !

Min. Oh, St. Jerome !—here is her father, and his privy counſellor, Gaſper. I can never communicate a ſecret in quiet. Well ! come to my chamber, for, now my hand's in, you ſhall have the whole.—I wou'd not keep it another day, to be confidant to an infanta.

[*Exeunt.*

Enter Don Cæsar *and* Gasper.

Gasp. Take comfort, Sir ; take comfort.

Cæs. *Take* it !—why where the devil ſhall I find it ? You may ſay, take phyſic Sir, or, take poiſon, Sir—— they are to be had ; but what ſignifies bidding me take comfort, when I can neither buy it, beg it, nor ſteal it ?

Gasp. But patience will bring it, Sir.

Cæs. 'Tis falſe, ſirrah.—Patience is a cheat, and the man that rank'd her with the cardinal virtues was a fool. —I have had patience at bed and board theſe three long years, but the comfort ſhe promis'd, has never called in with a civil how d'ye.

Gasp.

Gasp. Ay, Sir, but you know the poets fay that the twin fifter and companion of comfort is good humour.— Now if you would but drop that agreeable acidity, which is fo confpicuous——

Cæs. Then let my daughter drop her perverfe humour; 'tis a more certain bar to marriage than uglinefs or folly; and will fend me to my grave, at laft, without male heirs. [*crying.*] How many have laid fiege to her! But that humour of her's, like the works of Gibraltar, no Spaniard can find pregnable.

Gasp. Ay, well—Troy held out but ten years—— Let her once tell over her beads, *unmarried*, at five-and-twenty, and, my life upon it, fhe ends the rofary, with a hearty prayer for a good hufband.

Cæs. What, d'ye expect me to wait till the horrors of old maidenifm frighten her into civility? No, no;—I'll fhut her up in a convent, marry myfelf, and have heirs in fpite of her. There's my neighbour Don Vafquez's daughter, fhe is but nineteen——

Gasp. The very ftep I was going to recommend, Sir. You are but a young gentleman of fixty-three, I take it; and a hufband of fixty-three, who marries a wife of nineteen, will never want heirs, take my word for it.

Cæs. What! do you joke, firrah?

Gasp. Oh no, Sir—not if you are ferious. I think it would be one of the pleafanteft things in the world—Madam would throw a new life into the family; and when you are above ftairs in the gout, Sir, the mufic of her concerts, and the fpirit of her converzationes would reach your fick bed, and be a thoufand times more comforting than flannels and panada.

Cæs.

Cæs. Come, come, I underſtand ye.—But this daughter of mine—i ſhall give her but two chances more.——
Don Garcia and Don Vincentio will both be here to-day, and if ſhe plays over the old game, I'll marry to-morrow morning, if I hang myſelf the next.

Gasp. You decide right, Signor ; at ſixty-three the marriage nooſe and the hempen nooſe ſhould always go together.

Cæs. Why, you dog you, do you ſuppoſe—There's Don Garcia—there he is, coming through the portico. Run to my daughter, and bid her remember what I have ſaid to her. 　　　　　　　　　　[*Exit* Gasp.

She has had her leſſon—but another memento mayn't be amiſs—a young ſlut !—pretty, and witty, and rich— a match for a prince, and yet—but hiſt !——Not a word to my young man, if I can but keep him in ignorance 'till he is married, he muſt make the beſt of his bargain afterwards, as other honeſt men have done before him.

Enter Garcia.

Welcome, Don Garcia !—why you are rather before your time.

Garc. Gallantry forbid that I ſhould not, when a fair lady is concern'd. Should Donna Olivia welcome me as frankly as you do, I ſhall think I have been tardy.

Cæs. When you made your overtures, Signor, I underſtood it was from inclination to be allied to my family, not from a particular paſſion to my daughter. Have you ever ſeen her ?

Garc. But once—that tranſiently—yet ſufficient to convince me that ſhe is charming.

　　　　　　　　　　　　　　　　Cæs.

Cæs. Why yes, tho' I fay it, there are few prettier women in Madrid; and fhe has got enemies amongſt her own fex accordingly. They pretend to fay that——I fay, Sir, they have reported that fhe is not blefs'd with that kind of docility and gentlenefs that a —— now, tho' fhe may not be fo very placid, and infipid, as fome young women, yet, upon the whole—

Garc. Oh fye, Sir !—not a word—A beauty cannot be ill-temper'd ; gratified vanity keeps her in good humour with herfelf, and every body about her.

Cæs. Yes, as you fay—vanity is a prodigious fweet- ner ; and Olivia, confidering how much fhe has been hu- moured, is as gentle and pliant as——

Enter MINETTE.

Min. Oh, Sir ! fhield me from my miſtrefs—She is in one of her old tempers—the whole houfe is in an up- roar.—I cannot fupport it !

Cæs. ·Hufh !

Min. No, Sir, I can't hufh—A faint could not bear it. I am tired of her tyranny, and muſt quit her fervice.

Cæs. Then quit it in a moment— go to my ſteward, and receive your wages—go—begone ! 'Tis a coufin of my daughter's fhe is fpeaking of.

Min. A coufin, Sir !—No, 'tis Donna Olivia, your daughter—my miſtrefs. Oh, Sir ! you feem to be a fweet tender-hearted young gentleman—'twould move you to pity if—— [*to Garcia.*

Cæs. I'll move you, huffey, to fome purpofe, if you don't move off.

Garc. I am really confounded——can the charming Olivia——

Cæs.

Cæs. Spite, Sir—meer malice! My daughter has refus'd her some cast gown, or some—

OLIVIA *without.*

Where is she!—Where is Minette?

Cæs. Oh 'tis all over!—the tempest is coming,

Enter OLIVIA.

Oliv. Oh, you vile creature!—to speak to me!—
to answer me!—am I made to be answer'd?

Cæs. Daughter! Daughter! [*During the following
conversation he shews the most anxious impatience.*

Oliv. Because I threw my work-bag at her, she had
the insolence to complain; and, on my repeating it, said
she would not bear it.—Servants chuse what they shall
bear!

Min. When you are married, Ma'am, I hope your
husband will bear your humour, less patiently than I have
done.

Oliv. My husband!—dost think my husband shall
contradict my will? Oh, I long to set a pattern to those
milky wives, whose mean compliances degrade the sex.

Garc. Opportune! [*Aside.*

Oliv. The only husband on record who knew how to
treat a wife was Socrates; and tho' his lady was a Grecian,
I have some reason to believe her descendants match'd into
our family; and never shall my tame submission disgrace
my ancestry.

Garc. Heav'ns! why have you never curb'd this in-
temperate spirit, Don Cæsar?

Oliv. [*starting.*] Curb'd, Sir! talk thus to your groom
—curbs and bridles for a woman's tongue!

GARC.

GARC. Not for your's, lady, truly ! 'tis too late. But had the torrent, now fo overbearing, been taken at its fpring, it might have been ftem'd, and turn'd in gentle ftreamlets at the mafter's pleafure.

OLIV. A miftake, friend !—my fpirit, at its fpring, was too powerful for any mafter.

GARC. Indeed !—perhaps you may meet a Petruchio, gentle Catherine, yet.

OLIV. But no gentle Catherine will he find me, be-lieve it.——Catherine ! why fhe had not the fpirit of a roafted chefnut—a few big words, an empty oath, and a fcanty dinner, made her as fubmiffive as a fpaniel. My fire will not be fo foon extinguifhed—it fhall refift big words, oaths, and ftarving.

MIN. I believe fo indeed ; help the poor gentleman, I fay, to whofe fate you fall.

GARC. Don Cæfar, adieu ! My commiferation for your fate fubdues the refentment I fhould otherwife feel at your endeavouring to deceive me into fuch a marriage.

OLIV. Marriage ! oh mercy !—Is this Don Garcia ?

[Apart to Cæfar.

CÆS. Yes, termagant !

OLIV. O, what a misfortune ! Why did you not tell me it was the gentleman you defign'd to marry me to ? Oh, Sir ! all that is paft was in fport ; a contrivance be-tween my maid and me : I have no fpirit at all—I am as patient as poverty.

GARC. This mafk fits too ill on your features, fair lady : I have feen you *without* difguife, and rejoice in your ignorance of my name, fince, but for

that,

that, my peaceful home might have become the feat of perpetual difcord.

Min.   Aye, Sir, you would never have known what a quiet hour——

Oliv.   [*ftrikes her.*] Impertinence ! Indeed, Sir, I can be as gentle and forbearing as a pet lamb.

Garc.   I cannot doubt it, Madam ; the proofs of your placidity are very ftriking—But, adieu ! though I fhall pray for your converfion, rather than have the honour of it—I'd turn Dominican, and condemn myfelf to perpetual celibacy.   [*Exit.*

Cæs.   Now, huffey !—now, huffey !—what do you expect ?

Oliv.   Dear me ! how can you be fo unreafonable ! did ever daughter do more to oblige a father ! I abfolutely begg'd the man to have me.

Cæs.   Yes, vixen ! after you had made him deteft ye ; what, I fuppofe, he did not hit your fancy, madam ; tho' there is not in all Spain a man of prettier converfation.

Oliv.   Yes, he has a very pretty kind of converfation ; 'tis like a parenthefis.

Cæs.   Like a parenthefis !

Oliv.   Yes, it might be all left out, and never mifs'd. However, I thought him a modeft kind of a well-meaning young man, and that he would make a pretty fort of a hufband—for notwithftanding his bluftering, had I been his wife, in three months he fhould have been as humble and complaifant as——

Cæs.   Ay, there it is—there it is !—that fpirit of yours, huffey, you can neither conquer nor conceal ; but I'll find a way to tame it, I'll warrant me.   [*Exit.*
[*Olivia*

[*Olivia and Minette follow him with their eyes, and then burst into a laugh.*]

MIN. Well, madam, I give you joy ! had other ladies as much fuccefs in getting lovers, as you have in getting rid of yours, what contented faces we fhould fee.

OLIV. But to what purpofe do I get rid of them, whilft they rife in fucceffion like monthly pinks ? Was there ever any thing fo provoking ?—After fome quiet, and believing the men had ceafed to trouble themfelves about me, no lefs than two propofals have been made to my inexorable father this very day—What will become of me ?

MIN. What fhou'd become of you ? You'll chufe one from the pair, I hope. Believe me, madam, the only way to get rid of the impertinence of lovers, is to take one, and make him a fcare-crow to the reft.

OLIV. Oh, but I cannot !—Invention affift me this one day !

MIN. Upon my word, madam, invention owes you nothing ; and I am afraid you can draw on that bank no longer.—You muft truft to your eftablifhed character of vixen.

OLIV. But that won't frighten 'em all, you know, tho' it did its bufinefs with fober Don Garcia. The brave General Antonio would have made a property of me, in fpite of every thing, had I not luckily difcovered his antipathy to cats, and fo fcar'd the hero, by pretending an immoderate paffion for young kittens.

MIN. Yes, but you was ftill harder pufh'd by the Caftilian Count, and his engrav'd genealogy from Noah.

OLIV. Oh, he would have kept his poft as immovably as the griffins at his gate, had I not very ferioufly imparted to him, that my mother's great uncle fold oranges in Arragon.

ragon. Ha! ha! ha! And my little delicate fpark, who wafhes in rofe-water, and has his bed ftrewed with violets, would never have difmiffed himfelf, hadft thou not fcented my marefchal powder with affa fœtida.

Min. And pray, madam, if I may be fo bold, who is the next gentleman?

Oliv. Oh, Don Vincentio, who diftracts every body with his fkill in mufic. He ought to be married to a Viol de Gamba. I blefs my ftars I have never yet had a mifer in my lift—on fuch a character all art would be loft, and nothing but an earthquake, to fwallow up my eftate, could fave me.

Min. Well, if fome one did but know, how happy would fome one be, that for his fake——

Oliv. Now, don't be impertinent, Minette. You have feveral times attempted to flide yourfelf into a fecret, which I am refolv'd to keep to myfelf. Continue faithful, and fupprefs your curiofity. [*Exit.*

Min. Supprefs my curiofity, madam!—why, I am a chambermaid, and a forry one too, it fhould feem, to have been in your confidence two years, and never have got the mafter-fecret yet. I never was fix weeks in a family before, but I knew every fecret they had in it for three generations; aye, and I'll know this too, or I'll blow up all her plans, and declare to the world that fhe is no more a vixen than other fine ladies——they have moft of 'em a touch on't. [*Exit.*

END OF THE FIRST ACT.

A C T II. S C E N E I.

An Apartment at Donna LAURA's.

Enter LAURA *followed by* CARLOS.
CARLOS.

NAY, Madam, you may as well ſtop here, for I'll follow you through every apartment, but I will be heard. [*ſeizing her hand.*

LAU. This inſolence is not to be endured ; within my own walls to be thus——

CAR. The time has been, when within your walls I might be maſter.

LAU. Yes, you were then maſter of my heart, *that* gave you a right which——

CAR. You have now transferred to another. [*flinging away her hand.*]

LAU. Well, Sir !

CAR. " Well, Sir !"—Unbluſhing acknowledgment ! Falſe, fickle woman !

LAU. Becauſe I have luckily got the ſtart of you ; in a few weeks I ſhould have been the accuſer, and *you* the falſe and fickle.

CAR. And to ſecure yourſelf from that diſgrace, you prudently looked out in time for another lover.

LAU. I can pardon your ſneer, becauſe you are mortified.

CAR. Mortified !

LAU. Yes, mortified to the ſoul. Carlos ! I know your ſex : the vaineſt female, in the hour of her exultation and power, is ſtill out-done by man in vanity.—'Tis

C   more

more your ruling paſſion, than 'tis ours ; and 'tis wounded *vanity* that makes you thus tremble with rage at being deſerted.

CAR. [*Stamping*] Madam ! Madam !

LAU. This rage would have been all cool inſolence, had I waited for your change—the crime which now appears ſo black in me. Then, whilſt, with all my ſex's weakneſs, I had knelt at your feet, and reproached you only with my tears ; how *compoſed* would have been your feelings.—Scarcely would you have deigned to form a phraſe of pity for me ; perhaps have bid me forget a man no longer worthy my attachment, and recommended me to hartſhorn and my women.

CAR. Has any hour ſince I have firſt known you, given you cauſe for ſuch unjuſt ——

LAU. Yes, every hour—Now, Carlos, I bring thee to the teſt !—You ſaw, you lik'd, you lov'd me ; was there no fond truſting woman whom you deſerted to indulge the tranſient paſſion ? Yes, one bleſt with beauty, gentleneſs and youth ; one, who more than her own being lov'd thee, who made thee rich, and whom thou mad'ſt thy wife.

CAR. My wife !—here's a turn ! So to revenge the quarrels of my wife——

LAU. No, do not miſtake me—what I have done was merely to indulge myſelf, without more regard to your feelings, than you had to her's.

CAR. And you dare avow to my face, that you have a paſſion for another ?

LAU. I do, and—for I am above diſguiſe—I confeſs, ſo tender is my love for Florio, it has ſcarcely left a trace of that I once avow'd for Carlos.

CAR.

CAR. Well, Madam, if I hear this without some sudden vengeance on the tongue which speaks it, thank the annihilation of that passion, whose remembrance is as dead in my bosom as in yours. Let us, however, part friends, and with a mutual acquittal of every obligation—so give up the settlement of that estate, which left me almost a beggar.

LAU. Give it up!—ha, ha!——no, Carlos, you consign'd me that estate as a proof of love; do not imagine then, I'll give up the only part of our connection, of which I am not ashamed.

CAR. Base woman! you know 'twas not a voluntary gift—after having in vain practis'd on my fondness, whilst in a state of intoxication, you prevailed on me to sign the deed, which you had artfully prepar'd for the purpose—therefore, you must restore it.

LAU. Never, never.

CAR. Ruin is in the word!——Call it back, Madam, or I'll be reveng'd on thee in thy heart's dearest object—thy minion Florio!——*he* shall not riot on my fortune.

LAU. Ha, ha, ha! Florio is safe—your lands are sold, and in another country we shall enjoy the blessing of thy fond passion, whilst that passion is indulging itself in hatred and execrations. [*Exit.*

CAR. My vengeance shall first fall on her. [*following*] No, he shall be the first victim, or 'twill be incomplete.—Reduc'd to poverty, I cannot live;——Oh, folly! where are now all the gilded prospects of my youth? Had I——but 'tis too late to look back,—remorse attends the past, and ruin!—ruin waits me in the future!

S C E N E II.

Don Cæsar's.

Victoria *enters perusing a letter* ; *enter* Olivia.

Oliv. [*Speaks as entering*] To be sure—if my father should enquire for me, tell him I am in Donna Victoria's apartment.—Smiling, I protest ! my dear gloomy cousin, where have you purchased that fun-shiny look ?

Vict. It is but April sunshine, I fear ; but who could resist *such* a temptation to smile ? a letter from Donna Laura, my husband's mistress, stiling me her dearest Florio ! her life ! her soul ! and complaining of a twelve hours absence, as the bitterest misfortune.

Oliv. Ha, ha, ha ! most doughty Don ! pray let us see you in your feather and doublet ; as a Cavaleiro, it seems, you are formidable. So suddenly to rob your husband of his charmer's heart ! you must have us'd some witchery.

Vict. Yes, powerful witchery—the knowledge of my sex. Oh ! did the men but know us, as well as we do ourselves ;—but thank fate they do not, 'twould be dangerous.

Oliv. What, I suppose, you prais'd her understanding, was captivated by her wit, and absolutely struck dumb by the amazing beauties of——*her mind.*

Vict. Oh, no,—that's the mode prescribed by the *Essayists* on the female heart—ha, ha, ha !—Not a woman breathing, from fifteen to fifty, but would rather have a compliment to the tip of her ear, or the turn of her ancle, than a volume in praise of her intellects.

Oliv. So flattery then, is your boasted pill ?

Vict.

VICT. No, that's only the occafional gilding; but 'tis in vain to attempt a defcription of what changed its nature with every moment. I was now attentive—now gay—then tender—then carelefs. I ftrove rather to convince her that *I was charming*, than that I myfelf was charm'd; and when I faw love's arrow quivering in her heart, inftead of falling at her feet, fung a triumphant air, and remember'd a fudden engagement.

OLIV. [*Archly*] Would you have done fo, had you been a man?

VICT. Affuredly—knowing what I now do as a woman.

OLIV. But can all this be worth while, merely to rival a fickle hufband with one woman, whilft he is fetting his feather, perhaps, at half a fcore others?

VICT. To rival him was not my firft motive. The Portugueze robbed me of his heart; I concluded fhe had fafcinations which nature had denied to me; it was impoffible to vifit her as a woman; I, therefore, affumed the Cavalier to ftudy her, that I might, if poffible, be to my Carlos, all he found in her.

OLIV. Pretty humble creature!

VICT. In this adventure I learnt more than I expected;—my (oh cruel!) my hufband has given this woman an eftate, almoft all that his diffipations had left us.

OLIV. Indeed!

VICT. To make him more culpable, it was my eftate, it was that fortune which my lavifh love had made his, without fecuring it to my children.

OLIV. How could you be fo improvident?

VICT,

VICT. Alas! I trufted him with my heart, with my happinefs, *without* reftriction. Should I have fhewn a greater folicitude for any thing, than for thefe? [*weeps*

OLIV. The event proves that you fhould; but how can you be thus paffive in your forrow? fince I had affum'd the man, I'd make him feel a man's refentment for fuch injuries.

VICT. Oh, Olivia! what refentment can I fhew to him I have vow'd to honour, and whom, both my duty and my heart compel me yet to love?

OLIV. Why, really now, I think—pofitively, there's no thinking about it; 'tis among the arcana of the married life, I fuppofe.

VICT. You, who know me, can judge how I fuffered in profecuting my plan. I have thrown off the delicacy of fex; I have worn the mafk of love to the deftroyer of my peace—but the object is too great to be abandoned— nothing lefs than to fave my hufband from ruin, and to reftore him, again a lover, to my faithful bofom.

OLIV. Well, I confefs, Victoria, I hardly know whether moft to blame or praife you; but, with the reft of the world, I fuppofe, your fuccefs will determine me.

Enter GASPER.

GASP. Pray, Madam, are your wedding fhoes ready? [*to Olivia.*]

OLIV. Infolence! .... I can fcarcely ever keep up the vixen to this fellow. [*apart to Victoria.*]

GASP. You'll want them, Ma'am, to morrow morning, that's all—fo I came to prepare ye.

OLIV. *I* want wedding fhoes to-morrow! if you are kept on water gruel 'till I marry, that plump face of yours will be chap-fall'n, I believe.

GASP.

GASP. Yes, truly, I believe fo too. Lackaday, did you fuppofe I came to bring you news of your own wedding? no fuch glad tidings for you, lady, believe me.— You married! I am fure the man who ties himfelf to you, ought to be half a falamander, and able to live in fire.

OLIV. What marriage then is it, you do me the honour to inform me of?

GASP. Why, your father's marriage. You'll have a mother-in-law to-morrow, and having, like a dutiful daughter, danced at the wedding, be immur'd in a convent for life.

OLIV. Immur'd in a convent! then I'll raife fedition in the fifterhood, depofe the abbefs, and turn the confeffor's chair to a go-cart.

GASP. So the threat of the mother-in-law, which I thought would be worfe than that of the abbefs, does not frighten ye?

OLIV. No, becaufe my father dares not give me one. —Marry, without my confent! no, no, he'll never think of it, depend on't; however, left the fit fhould grow ftrong upon him, I'll go and adminifter my volatiles to keep it under. [*Exit.*

GASP. •Adminifter 'em cautioufly then—too ftrong a dofe of your volatiles would make the fit ftubborn. Who'd think that pretty arch look belong'd to a termagant? what a pity! 'twould be worth a thoufand ducats to cure her.

VICT. Has Inis told you I wanted to converfe with you in private, Gafper?

GASP. Oh, yes, madam, and I took particular notice that it was to be in private.——Sure, fays I, Mrs. Inis, Madam Victoria has not taken a fancy to me, and is going to break her mind.

VICT.

VICT. Whimfical! ha, ha! fuppofe I fhould, Gaf-per?

GASP. Why, then, madam, I fhould fay fortune had ufed you dev'lifh fcurvily, to give me a grey beard in a livery. I know well enough that fome young ladies have given themfelves to grey beards in a gilded coach, and others have run away with a handfome youth in worfted lace; they each had their apology; but if you run away with me—pardon me, madam, I could not ftand the ridicule.

VICT. Oh, very well; but if you refufe to run away with me, will you do me another favour?

GASP. Any thing you'll order, madam, except danc-ing a fandango.

VICT. You have feen my rich old uncle in the coun-try?

GASP. What, Don Sancho, who, with two-thirds of a century in his face, affects the mifdemeanors of youth; hides his baldnefs with amber locks, and com-plains of the tooth-ache, to make you believe that the two rows of ivory he carries in his head, grew there.

VICT. Oh, you know him, I find; could you affume his character for an hour, and make love for him? you know it muft be in the ftile of King Roderigo the Firft.

GASP. Hang it! I am rather too near his own age; to appear an old man with effect, one fhould not be above twenty; 'tis always fo on the ftage.

VICT. Pho! you might pafs for Juan's grandfon.

GASP. Nay, if your ladyfhip condefcends to flatter me, you have me.

VICT. Then follow me, for Don Cæfar, I hear, is approaching—in the garden I'll make you acquainted

with

with my plan, and impreſs on your mind every trait of my uncle's character. If you can hit him off, the arts of Laura ſhall be foil'd, and Carlos be again Victoria's.

[*Exit.*

Enter Don CÆSAR, *followed by* OLIVIA.

CÆS. No, no, 'tis too late—no coaxings; I am reſolv'd, I ſay.

OLIV. But it is not too late, and you ſhan't be reſolv'd, I ſay. Indeed, now, I'll be upon my guard with the next Don—what's his name? not a trace of the Xantippe left.—I'll ſtudy to be charming.

CÆS. Nay, you need not ſtudy it, you are always charming enough, if you would but hold your tongue.

OLIV. Do you think ſo? then to the next lover I won't open my lips; I'll anſwer every thing he ſays with a ſmile, and if he aſks me to have him, drop a court'ſey of thankfulneſs.

CÆS. Pſhaw! that's too much t'other way; you're always either above the mark or below it; you muſt talk, but talk with good humour. Can't you look gently and prettily, now, as I do? and ſay, " *yes, Sir,* and *no, Sir;* and *'tis very fine weather, Sir* ; and *pray, Sir, were you at the ball laſt night?* and *I caught a ſad cold the other evening* ; and, *bleſs me! I hear Lucinda has run away with her footman, and Don Philip has married his houſemaid.*"——That's the way agreeable ladies talk, you never hear any thing elſe.

OLIV. Very true; and you ſhall ſee me as agreeable as the beſt of 'em, if you won't give me a mother-in-law to ſnub me, and ſet me taſks, and to take up all the fine apartments, and ſend up your poor little Livy to lodge next the ſtars.

CÆS.

CÆs. Ha,——if thou wert but always thus foft and good-humour'd, no mother-in law in Spain, though fhe brought the Caftiles for her portion, fhould have power to fnub thee. But, Livy, the trial's at hand, for at this moment do I expeæt Don Vincentio to vifit you. He is but juft returned from England, and, probably, has yet heard only of your beauty and fortune; I hope it is not from you he will learn the other part of your charaæter.

Oliv. This moment expeæt him! two new lovers in a day?

CÆs. Beginning already, as I hope to live; aye, I fee 'tis in vain; I'll fend him an excufe, and marry Marcella before night.

Oliv. Oh, no! upon my obedience, I promife to be juft the foft civil creature you have defcribed.

Enter Servant.

Ser. Don Vincentio is below, Sir.

CÆs. I'll wait upon him——well, go and colleæt all your fmiles and your fimpers, and remember all I have faid to you ;—— be gentle, and talk pretty little fmall talk, d'ye hear, and if you pleafe him, you fhall have the portion of a Dutch burgomafter's daughter, and the pin-money of a princefs, you jade you. I think at laft I have done it; the fear of this mother-in-law will keep down the fiend in her, if any thing can.   [*Exit.*

Oliv. Hah! my poor father, your anxieties will never end 'till you bring Don Julio:——Command me to facrifice my *petulence*, my *liberty* to him, and Iphigenia herfelf, could not be more obedient. But what fhall I do with this Vincentio?—I fear he is fo perfeætly harmoniz'd, that to put him in an ill temper will be impraæti-
cable.——

cable.—I muſt try, however; if 'tis poſſible to find a diſ-
cord in him, I'll touch the ſtring. [*Exit.*

Another Apartment.

Enter VINCENTIO *and* CÆSAR.

VIN. Preſto, preſto, Signor! where is the Olivia?—
not a moment to ſpare. I left off in all the fury of compoſition; minums and crotchets have been battling it
through my head the whole day, and trying a ſemibreve in
G ſharp, has made me as flat as double F.

CÆS. Sharp and flat!—trying a ſemibreve!—oh—
gad, Sir! I had like not to have underſtood you; but a
ſemibreve is ſomething of a demi-culverin, I take it;
and you have been practiſing the art military.

VIN. Art military!—what, Sir! are you unacquaint-
ed with muſic?

CÆS. Muſic! oh I aſk pardon; then you are fond of
muſic——'ware of diſcords. [*aſide.*]

VIN. Fond of it! devoted to it.—I compos'd a thing
to-day in all the guſto of *Sachini* and the ſweetneſs of
Gluck. But this recreant finger fails me in compoſing a
paſſage in E, octave: if it does not gain more elaſtic
vigour in a week, I ſhall be tempted to have it amputated,
and ſupply the ſhake with a ſpring.

CÆS. Mercy! amputate a finger to ſupply a ſhake!

VIN. Oh, that's a trifle in the road to reputation—
to be talk'd of is the ſummum bonum of this life.——A
young man of rank ſhou'd not glide through the world
without a diſtinguiſh'd rage, or, as they call it in England
——a hobby horſe!

CÆS. A hobby horſe!

VIN.

Vin. Yes; that is, every man of figure determines on setting out in life, in that land of liberty, in what line to ruin himself; and that choice is called his *hobby horse*. One, makes the turf his scene of action—another drives about tall phætons to peep into their neighbour's garret windows; and a third rides his hobby horse in parliament, where it jerks him sometimes on one side, and sometimes on the other; sometimes in, and sometimes out, 'till at length he is jerk'd out of his honesty, and his constituents out of their freedom.

Cæs. Aye !——Well, 'tis a wonder that with such sort of hobby horses as these they should still outride all the world to the goal of glory. I wish we had a few of 'em to jerk Spain into some consideration.

Vin. This is all *cantable*; nothing to do with the subject of the piece, which is Donna Olivia ;——pray give me the key note to her heart.

Cæs. Upon my word, Signor—to speak in your own phrase—I believe that note has never yet been founded.— Ah ! here she comes ! look at her.——Isn't she a charming girl ?

Vin. Touching ! Musical I'll be sworn ! her very air is harmonious !

Cæs. [*aside.*] I wish thou may'st find her tongue so.

Enter Olivia, court'seys profoundly to each.

Daughter, receive Don Vincentio——his rank, fortune and merit, entitle him to be the heiress of a grandee ; but he is contented to become my son-in-law, if you can please him.   [*Olivia court'seys again.*

Vin. Please me ! she entrances me ! Her presence
thrills

thrills me like a cadenza of Pachierotti's, and every nerve
vibrates to the mufic of her looks.

Her ftep *andante* gently moves,
　　Pianos glance from either eye ;
　Oh how *largetto* is the heart,
　　That charms fo *forté* can defy !

Donna Olivia, will you be contented to receive me as a lover ?

OLIV.   Yes, Sir——No, Sir.

VIN.   Yes, Sir ; no, Sir ! bewitching timidity !

CÆS.   Yes, Sir, fhe's remarkably timid.——She's in
the right cue, I fee. [*afide.*]

VIN.   'Tis clear you have never travell'd——I fhall
be delighted to fhew you England.—You will there fee
how entirely timidity is banifh'd the fex.   You muft affect
a mark'd character, and maintain it at all hazards.

OLIV.   'Tis a very fine day, Sir.

VIN.   Madam !

OLIV.   I caught a fad cold the other evening.—Pray
was you at the ball laft night ?

VIN.   What ball, fair lady ?

OLIV.   Blefs me ! they fay Lucinda has run away with
her footman, and Don Philip has married his houfe-maid.
——Now am I not very agreeable ? [*apart to Cæfar.*]

CÆS.   Oh, fuch perverfe obedience !

VIN.   Really, Madam, I have not the honour to know
Don Philip and Lucinda——nor am I happy enough entirely to comprehend you.

OLIV.   No ! I only meant to be agreeable——but perhaps you have no tafte for pretty little fmall talk ?

VIN.   Pretty little fmall talk !

OLIV.   A *mark'd* character you admire ; fo do I ; I
doat on it.——I wou'd not refemble the reft of the world
in any thing.

VIN.

Vin. *My* tafte to the fiftieth part of a crotchet !—— We fhall agree admirably when we are married.

Vin. And *that* will be unlike the reft of the world, and therefore charming.

Cæs. [*afide.*] It will do ! I have hit her humour at laft——Why did'nt this young dog offer himfelf before ?

Oliv. I believe I have the honour to carry my tafte that way farther than you, Don Vincentio. Pray now, what is your ufual ftile in living ?

Vin. My winters I fpend in Madrid, as other people do. My fummers I drawl through at my caftle——

Oliv. As other people do !——and yet you pretend to tafte and fingularity, ha ! ha ! ha ! Good Don Vincentio, never talk of a *mark'd* character again.——Go into the country in July to fmell rofes and woodbines, when *every body* regales on their fragrance ! Now I wou'd rufticate only in winter, and my bleak caftle fhou'd be decorated with verdure and flowers, amidft the foft zephyrs of December.

Cæs. [*Afide.*] Oh, fhe'll go too far !

Oliv. On the leaflefs trees I wou'd hang green branches—the labour of filk worms, and therefore *natural*; whilft my rofe fhrubs and myrtles fhou'd be fcented by the firft perfumers in Italy——*Unnatural* indeed, but therefore fingular and ftriking.

Vin. Oh, charming !—You beat me where I thought myfelf the ftrongeft.——Wou'd they but eftablifh newf-papers here, to paragraph our fingularities, we fhou'd be the moft envied couple in Spain.

Cæs. [*Afide.*] By St. Anthony, he is as mad as fhe is.

Vin. What fay you, Don Cæfar ? Olivia and her winter garden, and I and my mufic.

Oliv.

OLIV. Mufic, did you fay ! Mufic ! I am paffionately fond of that !

CÆS. She has fav'd my life——I thought fhe was going to knock down his hobby horfe. [*afide.*]

VIN. You enchant me ! I have the fineft band in Madrid—My firft violin draws a longer bow than Giardini ; my clarinets, my viol de gamba——Oh you fhall have fuch concerts !

OLIV. Concerts ! Pardon me there——My paffion is a fingle inftrument.

VIN. That's carrying fingularity very far indeed ! I love a crafh ; fo does every body of tafte.

OLIV. But my tafte isn't like *every body's*—my nerves are fo particularly fine, that more than one inftrument overpowers them.

VIN. Pray tell me the name of that one : I am fure it muft be the moft elegant and captivating in the world.—I am impatient to know it.—We'll have no other inftrument in Spain, and I will ftudy to become its mafter, that I may woo you with its mufic. Charming Olivia ! tell me, is it a harpfichord ? a piano forte ? a pentachord? a harp ?

OLIV. You have it—you have it——a harp—yes, a Jew's harp, is to me the only inftrument.——Are you not charm'd with the delightful h—u—m of its bafe ! running on the ear like the diftant rumble of a ftate coach ? It prefents the idea of vaftnefs and importance to the mind. The moment you are its mafter—I'll give you my hand.

VIN. Da capo, Madam, da capo ! a *Jew's harp !!*

OLIV. Blefs me, Sir, don't I tell you fo ? Violins chill me—clarinets by fympathy hurt my lungs ; and, inftead

ſtead of maintaining a band under my roof, I wou'd not keep a ſervant who knew a baſſoon from a flute, or could tell whether he heard a jigg or a canzonetta.

Cæs. Oh thou perverſe one ; you know you love concerts—you know you do ! [*in great agitation.*]

Oliv. I deteſt 'em ! It's vulgar cuſtom that attaches people to the ſound of fifty different inſtruments at once ; 'twould be as well to talk on the ſame ſubject in fifty different tongues.   A band ! 'tis a mere olio of ſound ; I'd rather liſten to a three-ſtring'd guittar, ſerenading a ſempſtreſs in ſome neighbouring garret.

Cæs. Oh you !——Don Vincentio, this is nothing but perverſeneſs—wicked perverſeneſs.—Huſſey !—didn't you ſhake when you mention'd a garret ? didn't bread and water and a ſtep-mother come into your head at the ſame time ?

Vinc. Piano, piano, good Sir !   Spare yourſelf all farther trouble.   Should the Princeſs of Guzzarat, and all her diamond mines, offer themſelves, I wou'd not accept them in lieu of my band—a band that has half ruined me to collect.—I wou'd have allowed Donna Olivia a blooming garden in winter ; I wou'd even have procur'd barrenneſs and ſnow for her in the dog-days ;—but—to have my band inſulted !—to have my knowledge in muſic ſlighted !—to be rous'd from all the energies of compoſition by the drone of a Jew's harp !   I cannot breathe under the idea.

Cæs. Then—then you refuſe her, Sir ?

Vin. I cannot uſe ſo harſh a word—I *take my leave* of the lady—Adieu, Madam——I leave you to enjoy your ſolos, whilſt I fly to the raptures of a craſh.

[*Exit,*
Cæs.

CÆSAR *goes up to her and looks her in the face ; then goes off without speaking.*

OLIV. Mercy ! that filent anger is terrifying—I read a young mother-in-law, and an old lady abbefs, in every line of his face.

Enter VICTORIA.

OLIV. Well, you heard the whole, I fuppofe—heard poor unhappy me fcorn'd and rejected.

VICT. I heard you in imminent danger ; and expected Signor Da Capo wou'd have fnapp'd you up, in fpite of caprice and extravagance.

OLIV. Oh they charm'd inftead of fcaring him.——I foon found that my only chance was to fall acrofs *his* caprice.—Where is the philofopher who cou'd withftand that ?

VICT. But what, my good coufin, does all this tend to ?

OLIV. I dare fay you can guefs.—Penelope had never cheated her lovers with a never-ending web, had fhe not had an Ulyffes.

VICT. An Ulyffes ! what are you then married ?

OLIV. O, no, not yet !—but, believe me, my defign is not to lead apes ; nor is my heart an icicle.——If you choofe to know more, put on your veil, and flip with me through the garden to the Prado.

VICT. I can't indeed.—I am this moment going to drefs *en homme,* to vifit the impatient Portuguefe.

OLIV. Send an excufe—for pofitively you go with me. Heaven and earth ! I am going to meet *a man !*—whom I have been fool enough to dream and think of thefe two years, and I don't know that ever he thought of me in his life.

D

VICT.

VICT. Two years difcovering that?

OLIV. He has been abroad. The only time I ever faw him was at the Dutchefs of Medina's—there were a thoufand people; and he was fo elegant, fo carelefs, fo handfome!—In a word, though he fet off for France the next morning, by fome witchcraft or other, he has been before my eyes ever fince.

VICT. Was the impreffion mutual?

OLIV. He hardly notic'd me—I was then a bafhful thing, juft out of a convent, and fhrunk from obfervation.

VICT. Why, I thought you were going to meet him?

OLIV. To be fure——I fent him a command this morning to be at the Prado. I am determined to find out if his heart is engaged, and if it is——

VICT. You'll crofs your arms, and crown your brow with willows.

OLIV. No, pofitively, not whilft we have myrtles.— I wou'd prefer Julio, 'tis true, to all his fex; but if he is ftupid enough to be infenfible to me, I fhan't for that reafon pine like a girl, on chalk and oatmeal.——No, no; in that cafe, I fhall form a new plan, and treat my future lovers with more civility.

VICT. You are the only woman in love, I ever heard talk reafonably.

OLIV. Well, prepare for the Prado, and I'll give you a leffon againft your days of widowhood. Don't you wifh *this* the moment, Victoria? A pretty widow at four-and-

twenty

twenty has more fubjects and a wider empire than the firft monarch upon earth.—I long to fee you in your weeds.

VICT. Never may you fee them ! Oh, Olivia !—my happinefs, my life, depend on my hufband. The fond hope of ftill being united to him, gives me fpirits in my affliction, and enables me to fupport even the period of his neglect, with patience. [*Exeunt.*

END OF THE SECOND ACT.

ACT

ACT III.   SCENE I.

A LONG STREET.

Julio enters from a Garden Gate with precipitation ; a Servant within fastens the Gate.

JULIO.

YES, yes, bar the gate faft, Cerberus, left fome other curious traveller fhould ftumble on your confines.—— If ever I am fo caught again——

GARCIA enters, going haftily acrofs, JULIO feizes him.

Don Garcia, never make love to a woman in a veil.

GARC. Why fo, prithee ? Veils and fecrecy are the chief ingredients in a Spanifh amour ; but in two years, Julio, thou art grown abfolutely French.

JULIO. That may be ; but if ever I truft to a veil again, may no lovely, blooming beauty ever truft me.— Why doft know I have been an hour at the feet of a creature whofe firft birth-day muft have been kept the latter end of the laft century, and whofe trembling, weak voice, I miftook for the timid cadence of bafhful fifteen!

GARC. Ha, ha, ha!—What a happinefs to have feen thee in thy raptures, petitioning for half a glance only, of the charms the envious veil conceal'd.

JULIO. Yes ; and when fhe unveil'd her Gothic countenance, to render the thing compleatly ridiculous, fhe began moralizing ; and pofitively would not let me out of the fnare, 'till I had perfuaded her fhe had work'd a converfion, verſion, and that I'd never make love—but in an *honeſt* way again.

GARC. Oh, that honeſt way of love-making is delightful, to be ſure. I had a doſe of it this morning ; but happily the ladies have not yet learnt to veil their tempers, though they have their faces.

Enter VINCENTIO.

VIN. Julio ! Garcia ! congratulate me !——Such an eſcape !

JULIO. *What* have you eſcap'd ?

VIN. Matrimony.

GARC. Nay, then our congratulations may be mutual.—I have had a matrimonial eſcape too, this very day. I was almoſt on the brink of the ceremony with the verieſt Xantippe !

VIN. Oh, that was not my caſe—mine was a ſweet creature, all elegance, all life.

JULIO. Then where's the cauſe of congratulation ?

VIN. Cauſe—why ſhe's ignorant of muſic ! prefers a jig to a canzonetta, and a Jew's harp to a pentachord.

JULIO. Jews harp !—Pho, prithee.

GARC. Had my nymph no other fault, I would pardon that, for ſhe was lovely and rich.

VIN. Mine too was lovely and rich, and, I'll be ſworn, as ignorant of ſcolding as of the gama ;—but not to know muſic !—

JULIO. Gentle, lovely, and rich—and ignorant *only* of muſic ?

GARC. A venial crime indeed ! if the ſweet creature will marry me, ſhe ſhall carry a Jew's harp always in he train, as a Scotch laird does his bagpipes. I wiſh you'd give me your intereſt.

D 3   VIN

Vin. Oh, moſt willingly, if thou haſt ſo groſs an inclination;—I'll name thee as a dull-ſoul'd, *largo* fellow, to
her father, Don Cæſar.

Garc. Cæſar! what Don Cæſar?

Vin. De Zuniga.

Garc. Impoſſible!

Vin. Oh, I'll anſwer for her mother. So much is De
Zuniga her father, that he does not know a ſemibreve from
a culverin.

Garc. The name of the lady?

Vin. Olivia.

Garc. Why you muſt be mad—that's my termagant.

Vin. Termagant!—ha! ha! ha! Thou haſt certainly ſome vixen of a miſtreſs, who infects thy ears towards the whole ſex. Olivia is timid and elegant.

Garc. By Juno, there never exiſted ſuch a ſcold.

Vin. By Orpheus, there never was a gayer temper'd
creature—Spirit enough to be charming, that's all. If ſhe
lov'd harmony, I'd marry her to morrow.

Julio. Ha, ha! what a ridiculous jangle! 'Tis evi-
dent you ſpeak of two different women.

Garc. I ſpeak of Donna Olivio, heireſs to Don Cæſar de Zuniga.

Vin. *I* ſpeak of the heireſs of Don Cæſar de Zuniga,
who is called Donna Olivia.

Garc. Sir, I perceive you mean to inſult me.

Vin. Your perceptions are very rapid, Sir—but if you
chuſe to think ſo, I'll ſettle that point with you immedi-
ately—But, for fear of conſequences, I'll fly home, and
add the laſt bar to my concerto, and then meet you where
you pleaſe.

Jul.

JULIO. Pho ! this is evidently misapprehenfion.—To clear the matter up, I'll visit the lady—if you'll introduce me, Vincentio ;—but you shall both promise to be govern'd in this difpute by my decifion.

VIN. I'll introduce you with joy, if you'll try to perfuade her of the neceffity of mufic, and the charms of harmony.

GARC. Yes, she needs that——You'll find her all jar and difcord.

JULIO. Come, no more Garcia—thou art but a fort of a male vixen thyfelf.—Melodious Vincentio, when shall I expect you ?

VIN. This evening.

JULIO. Not this evening ; I have engag'd to meet a goldfinch in a grove, then I shall have mufic, you rogue !

VIN. It won't fing at night.

JULIO. Then I'll talk to it till the morning, and hear it pour out its matins to the rifing fun.——Call on me tomorrow, I'll then attend you to Donna Olivia, and declare faithfully the impreffion her character makes on me. —Come, Garcia, I muft not leave you together, left his crotchets and your minums, should fall into a crash of difcords.   •   [*Exeunt oppofite fides.*

THE PRADO.

Enter CARLOS.

CAR. All hail to the powers of Burgundy ! Three flafks to my own share.—What forrows can ftand again three flafks of Burgundy ? I was a damn'd melanchol fellow this morning, going to shoot myfelf to get rid of my troubles.—Where are my troubles now ? Gone to the moon to look for my wits ; and there, I hope, they'll re-

main

main together, if one cannot come back without t'other.—
But where is this indolent dog, Julio ? *He* fit to receive
appointments from ladies ! Sure I have not mifs'd the
hour——No—but feven yet—[*looking at his watch.*]——
Seven's the hour, by all the joys of Burgundy ! The
rogue muft be here——let's reconnoitre.

Enter VICTORIA *and* OLIVIA, *veil'd, from the top.*

OLIV. Pofitively, mine's a pretty fpark, to let me be
firft at the place of appointment. I have half refolv'd to
go home again to punifh him.

VICT. I'll anfwer for its being but *half* a refolution—
to make it entire would be to punifh yourfelf.——There's
a folitary man—Is not that he ?

OLIV. I think not.——If he'd pleafe to turn his face
this way—

VICT. That's impoffible, while the loadftone is the
other way.——He is looking at the woman in the next
walk   Can't you difturb him ?

OLIV. [*Screams.*]   Oh ! a frightful frog !

[*Carlos turns.*

VICT. Heav'ns, 'tis my hufband.

OLIV. Your hufband ! Is that Don Carlos ?

VICT. It is indeed.

OLIV. Why really, now I fee the man, I don't wonder that you are in no hurry for your weeds.——He is
moving towards us.

VICT. I cannot fpeak to him, and yet my foul flies to
meet him.

CAR. Pray, lady, what occafioned that pretty fcream ?
I fhrewdly fufpect it was a trap.

OLIV. A trap ! Ha ! ha ! ha !—a trap *for you !*

CAR.

CAR. Why not, Madam ?—Zounds, a man fix feet high, and three flafks of Burgundy in his head, is worth laying a trap for.

OLIV. Yes, unlefs he happens to be trapp'd before.— 'Tis about two years fince you was caught, I take it—— Do keep farther off !——Odious ! a *married* man !

CAR. The devil ! Is it pofted under every faint in the ftreet, that I am a married man ?

OLIV. No, you carry the marks about you ; that rueful phiz could never belong to a batchelor.——Befides, there's an odd appearance on your temples—does your hat fit eafily ?

CAR. By all the thorns of matrimony, if——

OLIV. Poor man ! how natural to fwear by what one feels—but why were you in fuch hafte to gather the thorns of matrimony ? Blefs us ! had you but look'd about you a little, what a market might have been made of that fine, proper promifing perfon of yours——

CAR. Confound thee, confound thee ! If thou art a wife, may thy hufband plague thee with jealoufies, and thou never be able to give him caufe for them ; and if thou art a maid, may'ft thou be an *old* one ! [*Going, meets Julio.*] Oh, Julio, look not that way ; there's a tongue will ftun thee.

JULIO. Heav'n be prais'd ! I love female prattle. A woman's tongue can never fcare me.—Which of thefe two goldfinches makes the mufic ?

CAR. Oh, this is as filent as a turtle—[*taking Victoria's hand.*—only coos now and then.—Perhaps *you* don't hate a married man, fweet one ?

VICT. You guefs right ; *I* love a married man.

CAR.

CAR. Hah, fay'ft thou fo! wilt thou love me?

VICT. Will you let me?

CAR. Let thee, my charmer! how I'll cherifh thee for't.—What would I not give for thy heart!

VICT. I demand a price that, perhaps, you cannot give—I afk unbounded love; but you have a wife.

CAR. And, therefore, the readier to love every other woman;—'tis in your favour child.

VICT. Will you love me ever?

CAR. Ever! yes ever, 'till we find each other dull company, and yawn, and talk of our neighbours for amufement.

VICT. Farewell! I fufpected you to be a bad chapman, and that you would not reach my terms.   [going

CAR. Nay, I'll come to your terms if I can;—but move this way;—I am fearful of that wood-pecker at your elbow—fhould fhe begin again, her noife will fcare all the pretty loves that are playing about my heart. Don't turn your head towards them; if you like to liften to love tales, you'll meet fond pairs enough in this walk.

[forcing her gently off.

JULIO. I really believe, though you deny it, that you are my deftiny—that is, you fated me hither.—See, is not this your mandate?   [taking a letter from his pocket

OLIV. Oh, delightful! the fcrawl of fome chambermaid, or, perhaps, of your valet to give you an air—what is it figned? Marriatornes? Tomafa? Sancha?

JULIO. Nay, now I am convinced the letter is yours, fince you abufe it; fo you may as well confefs.

OLIV. Suppofe I fhould, you can't be fure that I do not deceive you.

JULIO. True; but there is one point in which I have made a vow not to be deceived; therefore, the preliminary is, that you throw off your veil.

OLIV.

OLIV. My veil !

JULIO. Positively ! if you reject this article, our nego-
ciation ends.

OLIV. You have no right to offer articles, unless you
own yourself conquered.

JULIO. I own myself willing to be conquer'd, and
have, therefore, a right to make the best terms I can.—
Do you accede to the demand ?

OLIV. Certainly not.

JULIO. You had better.

OLIV. I protest I will not.

JULIO. [*Aside*] My life upon't I make you. Why,
madam, how absurd this is—'tis reducing us to the situa-
tion of Pyramus and Thisbe, talking through a wall ;—yet
'tis of no consequence, for I know your features, as well
as though I saw 'em.

OLIV. How can that be ?

JULIO. I judge of what you hide, by what I see—I
could draw your picture.

OLIV. Charming ! pray begin the portrait.

JULIO. Imprimis, a broad high forehead, rounded at
the top, like an old-fashion'd gateway.

OLIV. Oh, horrid !

JULIO. Little grey eyes, a sharp nose, and hair, the
colour of rusty prunella.

OLIV. Odious !

JULIO Pale cheeks, thin lips, and——

OLIV. Hold, hold, thou villifier. [*throws off her veil,
be sinks on one knee*] There ! yes, kneel in contrition for
your malicious libel.

JULIO. Say rather, in adoration.—What a charming
creature !

OLIV.

OLIV. So, now for lies on the other fide.

JULIO. A forehead form'd by the Graces; hair, which Cupid would fteal for his bow ftrings, were he not engag'd in fhooting through thofe fparkling hazel circlets, which nature has given you for eyes; lips! that 'twere a fin to call fo—they are frefh gather'd rofe leaves, with the fragrant morning dew, ftill hanging on their rounded furface.

OLIV. Is that extemporaneous, or ready cut, for every woman who takes off her veil to you.

JULIO. I believe 'tis *not* extemporaneous, for nature, when fhe finifh'd you, form'd the fentiment in my heart, and there it has been hid, 'till you, for *whom* it was form'd, called it into words.

OLIV. Suppofe I fhould underftand, from all this, that you have a mind to be in love with me; wouldn't you be finely caught?

JULIO. Charmingly caught! if you'll let me underftand, at the fame time, that you have a mind to be in love with me.

OLIV. In love with a man! heavens! I never lov'd any thing but a fquirrel!

JULIO. Make me your fquirrel—I'll put on your chain, and gambol and play for ever at your fide.

OLIV. But fuppofe you fhould have a mind to break the chain?

JULIO. Then loofen it; for, if once that humour feizes me, reftraint won't cure it.—Let me fpring and bound at liberty, and when I return to my lovely miftrefs, tired of all but her, faften me again to your girdle, and kifs me while you chide,

OLIV. Your fervant—to encourage you to leave me again.

JULIO,

Julio. No, to make *returning* to you, the ſtrongeſt attraction of my life.—Why are you ſilent?

Oliv. I am debating whether to be pleaſed or diſpleaſed at what you have ſaid.

Julio. Well?

Oliv. You ſhall know when I have determined. My friend and yours are approaching this way, and they muſt not be interrupted.

Julio. 'Twou'd be barbarous—we'll retire as far off as you pleaſe.

Oliv. But we retire ſeparately, Sir,—that lady is a woman of honour, and this moment of the higheſt importance to her. You may, however, conduct me to the gate, on condition that you leave me inſtantly.

Julio. Leave her inſtantly—oh, then I know my cue. [*Exit together at top.*

Enter CARLOS, *followed by* VICTORIA, *unveiled.*

Car. [*Looking back on her*] My wife!

Vict. Oh, heavens! I will veil myſelf again. I will hide my face for ever from you, if you will ſtill feaſt my ears with thoſe ſoft vows, which a moment ſince you poured forth ſo eagerly.

Car. My wife!—making love to my own wife!

Vict. Why ſhould one of the deareſt moments of my life, be to you ſo diſpleaſing.

Car. So, I am caught in this ſnare, by way of *agreeable* ſurprize, I ſuppoſe.

Vict. Wou'd you cou'd think it ſo.

Car. No, madam! by heav'n 'tis a ſurprize fatal to every hope with which you may have flattered yourſelf.— What am I to be followed, haunted, watched?

Vict. Not to upbraid you.—I follow'd you, becauſe

my

my caſtle without you ſeem'd a dreary deſart.—Indeed,
I will never upbraid you.

CAR. Generous aſſurance !—never upbraid me—no
by heavens, I'll take care you never ſhall.—She has
touch'd my ſoul, but I dare not yield to the impreſſion.—
Her ſoftneſs is worſe than death to me.   [aſide

VICT. Would I could find words to pleaſe you !

CAR. You cannot ; therefore leave me, or ſuffer me
to go without attempting to follow me.

VICT. Is it poſſible yoo can be ſo barbarous ?

CAR. Do not expoſtulate ; your firſt vow'd duty is
obedience—that word ſo grating to your ſex.

VICT. To me it was never grating—to obey you has
been my joy ; even now I will not diſpute your will,
though I feel, for the firſt time, obedience hateful. [going,
and then turning back] Oh, Carlos ! my dear Carlos ! I
go, but my ſoul remains with you.   [Exit.

CAR. Oh, horrible ! had I not taken this harſh mea-
ſure, I muſt have kill'd myſelf, for how could I tell her
that I have made her a beggar ? better ſhe ſhould hate,
deteſt me ! than that my tenderneſs ſhould give her a
proſpect of felicity, which now ſhe can never taſte.——
Oh, wine-created ſpirit ! Where art thou now ? Madneſs,
return to me again ; for reaſon preſents me nothing but
deſpair.

Enter JULIO, from the top.

JULIO. Carlos, who the devil can they be ? my
charming little witch was inflexible.——I hope yours has
been more communicative.

CAR. Folly !—Nonſenſe !   [Exit.

JULIO. Folly !—Nonſenſe ! What, a pretty woman's
ſmile ! ha, ha, ha ! upon my ſoul it has more perſuaſion,
and, conſequently, more reaſon, than a logical diſquiſition
          —but

—but thefe married fellows have neither tafte nor joy.—
Humph—fuppofe my fair one fhould want to debafe me into
fuch an animal;—fhe can't have fo much villainy in her
difpofition: and yet, if fhe fhould? pho! it won't bear
thinking about.—If I do fo mad a thing, it muft be as
cowards fight, without daring to reflect on the danger.

Scene, an apartment in the Houfe of Don VASQUEZ, MAR-
CELLA'S *Father.*

Enter CÆSAR *and* VASQUEZ.

CÆS. Well, Don Vafquez, and a——you——then I
fay, you have a mind that I fhould marry your daughter?

VASQ. It is fufficient, Signor, that you have fignified
to us your intention—my daughter fhall prove her gratitude, in her attention to your felicity.

CÆS. Egad! now it comes to the pufh! [*afide*] hem,
hem!—but juft nineteen, you fay.

VASQ. Exactly, the eleventh of laft month.

CÆS. Pity it was not twenty.

VASQ. Why a year can make no difference, I fhould
think.

CÆS. O, yes it does; a year's a great deal;—they
are fo fkittifh at nineteen.

VASQ. Thofe who are fkittifh at nineteen, I fear, you
won't find much mended at twenty. Marcella is very
grave, and a pretty little, plump, fair——

CÆS. Aye, fair, again! pity fhe isn't brown or olive
—I like your olives.

VASQ. Brown and olive! you are very whimfical, my
old friend.

CÆS. Why thefe fair girls are fo ftared at by the men,
and the young fellows, now-a-days, have a damn'd im-

pudent

pudent ftare with them,—'tis very abafhing to a woman—
very diftreffing !

VASQ. Yes, fo it is; but happily their diftrefs is of
that nature that it generally goes off in a fimper. But
come, I'll fend Marcella to you, and fhe will——

CÆS. No, no, ftay my good friend. [*gafping*] You
are in a violent hurry.

VASQ. Why, truly, Signor, at our time of life,
when we determine to marry, we have no time to lofe.

CÆS. Why, that's very true, and fo—oh! St. Anthony, now it comes to the point—but there can be no
harm in looking at her—a look won't bind us for better
for worfe. [*afide*] Well then—if you have a mind, I fay,
you may let me fee her. *Exit Vafquez.*

CÆS. [*Puts on his fpectacles*] Aye, here fhe comes—
I hear her—trip, trip, trip! I don't like that ftep. A
woman fhould always tread fteadily, with dignity, it
awes the men.

Enter VASQUEZ, *leading* MARCELLA.

VASQ. There, Marcella, behold your future hufband; and remember that your kindnefs to him, will be
the ftandard of your duty to me. *Exit.*

MARC. Oh, heavens! [*afide*

CÆS. Somehow I am afraid to look round.

MARC. Surely he does not know that I am here!
[*coughs gently.*

CÆS. So——fhe knows how to give an item, I find.

MARC. Pray, Signor, have you any commands for
me?

CÆS. Hum!—not non plus'd at all. [*looks around*]
Oh! that eye, I don't like that eye.

MARC.

MARC. My father commanded me——

CÆS. Yes, I know—I know. [*to her*] Why, now I look again, there is a fort of a modeft.—Oh, that fmile! that fmile will never do. [*afide.*

MARC. I underftand, Signor, that you have demanded my hand in marriage.

CÆS. Upon my word, plump to the point! [*afide*] Yes, I did a fort of—I can't fay but that I did——

MARC. I am not infenfible of the honour you do me, Sir, but—but——

CÆS. But!—What don't you like the thoughts of the match?

MARC. Oh, yes, Sir, yes—exceedingly. I dare not fay no. [*afide.*

CÆS. Oh, you do—*exceedingly*! What, I fuppofe, child, your head is full of jewels, and finery, and equipage? [*with ill humour.*

MARC. No indeed, Sir.

CÆS. No, what then? what fort of a life do you expect to lead when you are my wife? what pleafures d'ye look forward to?

MARC. None!

CÆS. Hey!

MARC. I fhall obey my father, Sir; I fhall marry you; but I fhall be moft wretched! [*weeps*

CÆS. Indeed!

MARC. There is not a fate I would not prefer;—but pardon me!

CÆS. Go on, go on, I never was better pleas'd

MARC. Pleas'd at my reluctance!

CÆS. Never, never better pleas'd in my life;—fo you had really now, you young baggage, rather have me for a grandfather than a hufband?

E MARC.

MARC. Forgive my franknefs, Sir,—a thoufand times !

CÆS. My dear girl, let me kifs your hand.—Egad ! you've let me off charmingly. I was frightened out of my wits left *you* fhould have taken as violent an inclination to the match, as your father has.

MARC. Dear Sir, you charm me.

CÆS. But hark ye;—you'll certainly incur your father's anger, if I don't take the refufal *entirely* on my-felf, which I will do, if you'll only affift me in a little bufinefs I have in hand.

MARC. Any thing to fhew my gratitude.

CÆS. You muft know, I can't get my daughter to marry—there's nothing on earth will drive her to it, but the dread of a mother-in-law. Now, if you will let it appear to her, that you and I are driving to the goal of matrimony; I believe it will do—what fay you? fhall we be lovers in play ?

MARC. If you are fure it will be *only* in play.

CÆS. Oh, my life upon't—but we muft be very fond, you know.

MARC. To be fure—exceedingly tender ; ha, ha, ha !

CÆS. You muft fmile upon me now and then roguifhly ; and flide your hand into mine, when you are fure fhe fees you, and let me pat your cheek, and——

MARC. Oh, no farther pray—that will be quite fuf-ficient.

CÆS. Gad, I begin to take a fancy to your rogue's face, now I'm in no danger—mayn't we—mayn't we fa-lute fometimes, it will feem infinitely more natural.

MARC. Never ; fuch an attempt would make me fly off at once.

CÆS. Well, you muft be lady governefs in this bu-finefs.—

fineſs.—I'll go home now, and fret madam, about her young mother-in-law—By'e ſweeting!

MARC. By'e charmer!

CÆS. Oh, bleſs its pretty eyes!   [*Exit.*

MARC. Bleſs its pretty ſpectacles! ha, ha, ha! enter into a league with a croſs old father againſt a daughter! why how could he ſuspect me capable of ſo much treachery? I cou'd not anſwer it to my conſcience. No, no I'll acquaint Donna Olivia with the plot; and, as in duty bound, we'll turn our arms againſt Don Cæſar.

        [*Exit.*

END OF THE THIRD ACT.

ACT IV.   SCENE I.

DONNA LAURA'S.

Enter LAURA *and* PEDRO.

LAURA.

WELL, Pedro ! haft thou feen Don Florio ?

PED. Yes, Donna.

LAU. How did he look when he read my letter ?

PED. Mortal well, I never fee'd him look better—he'd got on a new cloak, and a——

LAU. Pho, blockhead ! did he look pleas'd ? did he kifs my name ? did · he prefs the billet to his bofom with all the warmth of love ?

PED. No, he didn't warm it that way ; but he did another, for he put it into the fire.

LAU. How !

PED. Yes, and when I fpoke, he ftarted, for, I think, he had forgot that I was by—fo, fays he, go home and tell Donna Laura, I fly to her prefence.

[She waves her hand for him to go.]

LAU. Is it poffible ? fo contemptuoufly deftroy the letter in which my whole heart overflow'd with tendernefs ? in which my upbraidings were mingled with the moft paffionate love ! But why do I queftion it ? has he ever treated me but with the moft mortifying coldnefs, even whilft he pretended to be fenfible of my charms ? I feel myfelf on the brink of hatred ; and, by all the

agonies

agonies I have felt, fhou'd that paffion be once rous'd.—
Oh, how idly I talk! he is here; his very voice pierces
my heart. I dare not meet his eye thus difcompofed.

Exit.

Enter VICTORIA, *(in Men's Cloaths) preceded by* SANCHA.

SANCH. I will inform my miftrefs that you are here,
Don Florio, I thought fhe had been in this apartment.

Exit.

VICT. Now muft I, with a mind torn by anxities,
once more affume the lover of my hufband's miftrefs—of
the woman who has robb'd me of his heart, and his children of their fortune. Sure my tafk is hard.—Oh, love!
Oh, *married* love affift me! If I can, by any art, obtain
from her that fatal deed, I fhall fave my little ones from
ruin—and then——But I hear her ftep—[*agitated, preffing
her hand on her bofom*].——There! I have hid my griefs
within my heart, and now for all the impudence of an
accomplifhed cavalier!

[*Sings an air——fets her hat in the glafs——dances a few
fteps, &c. then runs to Laura, and feizes her hand.*]

VICT. My lovely Laura!

LAU. That look fpeaks Laura *lov'd* as well as lovely.

VICT. To be fure! Petrarch immortaliz'd *his* Laura
by his verfes, and mine fhall be immortal in my paffion.

LAU. I cannot conceive how you feed this immortal
paffion.

VICT. Oh, by thinking of you, and reading your
letters, and——

LAU. My letters! how often do you read them?

VICT. A dozen times an hour; drink each dear line
with my eyes, whilft my lips drink chocolate; place them
every night under my pillow, and——

E 3　　　　　　　　　　　　　　LAU.

LAU. In the morning fling them into the fire.

VICT. Madam!

LAU. Oh, Florio, how deceitful! I know not what inchantment binds me to thee.

VICT. Me! my dear! is all this to me? [*playing carelefly with the feather in her hat*]

LAU. Yes, ingrate, thee!

VICT. Pofitively, Laura, you have thefe extravagancies fo often, I wonder my paffion can ftand them. To be plain, thofe violences in your temper may make a pretty relief in the flat of matrimony, child, but they do not fuit that ftate of freedom which is neceffary to *my* happinefs.—It was by fuch deftructive arts as thefe you cured Don Carlos of his love.

LAU. *Cured* Don Carlos! Oh, Florio! wer't thou but as he is!

VICT. Why, you don't pretend he loves you ftill?

[*eagerly* ·

LAU. Yes, moft ardently and truly.

VICT. Hah!

LAU. If thou would'ft perfuade me that thy paffion is real, borrow *his* words, *his* looks;—be a hypocrite one dear moment, and fpeak to me in all the frenzy of that love, which warms the heart of Carlos.

VICT. The heart of Carlos!

LAU. Hah, that feem'd a jealous pang—it gives my hopes new life. [*afide*] Yes, Florio, he, indeed, knows what it is to love.—For me he forfook a beauteous wife; nay, and *with* me he wou'd forfake his country.

VICT. Villain! Villain!

LAU. Nay, let not the thought diftrefs you thus;—Carlos I defpife—he is the weakeft of mankind.

VICT.

VICT. 'Tis falſe, madam, you cannot deſpiſe him—
Carlos the weakeſt of mankind! heavens! what woman
cou'd reſiſt him? Perſuaſion ſits on his tongue, and love,
almighty love, triumphant in his eyes!

LAU. This is ſtrange; you ſpeak of your rival with
the admiration of a miſtreſs.

VICT. Laura! it is the fate of jealouſy, as well as
love, to ſee the charms of its object, increaſ'd and heigh-
ten'd.—*I* am jealous,—jealous to diſtraction, of Don
Carlos, and cannot taſte peace, unleſs you'll ſwear never
to ſee him more. — How nearly had I been betray'd! [*aſide.*

LAU. I ſwear, joyfully ſwear, never to behold or
ſpeak to him again. When, dear youth! ſhall we retire
to Portugal? we are not ſafe here.

VICT. You know I am not rich.—You muſt firſt ſell
the lands my rival gave you. [*obſerving her with apprehenſion*

LAU. 'Tis done—I have found a purchaſer, and to-
morrow the transfer will be finiſhed.

VICT. [*Aſide*] Ah! I have now then nothing to truſt
to but the ingenuity of Gaſper.—There is reaſon to fear
Don Carlos had no right in that eſtate, with which you
ſuppoſed yourſelf endow'd.

LAU. No right! what can have given you thoſe ſuſ-
picions? •

VICT. A converſation with Juan his ſteward—who
aſſures me that his maſter never had an eſtate in Leon.

LAU. Never! what not by marriage?

VICT. Juan ſays ſo.

LAU. My blood runs cold—can I have taken pains
to deceive myſelf—cou'd I think ſo I ſhould be mad.

VICT. Theſe doubts may ſoon be annihilated; or con-

firm'd

firm'd to certainty.—I have seen Don Sancho, the uncle of Victoria—he is now in Madrid—You have told me that he once profess'd a passion for you.

LAU. Oh, to excess ; but at that time I had another object.

VICT. Have you convers'd with him much ?

LAU. I never saw him nearer than from my Balcony, where he used to ogle me through a glass, suspended by a ribbon, like an order of knighthood ; he is weak enough to fancy it gives him an air of distinction, ha, ha ! But where can I find him ? I must see him.

VICT. Write him a billet, and I will send it to his lodgings.

LAU. Instantly.—Dear Florio, a new prospect opens to me—Don Sancho is rich and generous ; and, by playing on his passions, without yielding to them, his fortune may be a constant fund to us.——I'll dip my pen in flattery.

[*Exit.*

VICT. Base woman ! how can I pity thee, or regret the steps which my duty obliges me to take ? For myself, I wou'd not swerve from the nicest line of rectitude, nor wear the shadow of deceit——But for my children ! ——Is there a parental heart that will not pardon me ?

[*Exit.*

SCENE, DON CÆSAR'S.

Enter OLIVIA *and* MINETTE

OLIV. Well, here we are in private—what is this charming intelligence of which thou art so full this morning ?

MIN. Why, Ma'am, as I was in the balcony that overlooks Don Vasquez's garden—Donna Marcella told me, me, that Don Cæfar had laft night been to pay her a vifit previous to their marriage, and——

OLIV. Their marriage! How can you give me the intelligence with fuch a look of joy? Their marriage! —what will become of me?

MIN. Dear, Ma'am! if you'll but have patience.—— She fays that Don Cæfar and fhe are perfectly agreed.——

OLIV. Still with that fmirking face——I can't have patience.

MIN. Then, Madam, if you won't let me tell the ftory, pleafe to read it——here's a letter from Donna Marcella.

OLIV. Why did you not give it me at firft? [reads.

MIN. Becaufe I did'nt like to be cut out of my ftory. If orators were oblig'd to come to the point at once, mercy on us! what tropes and figures we fhou'd lofe!

OLIV. Oh, Minette! I give you leave to fmirk again —liften—[reads.] "I am more terrified at the idea of be-
" coming your father's wife, than you are in the expect-
" ation of a ftep-mother; and Don Cæfar would be as
" loth as either of us.—He only means to frighten you
" into matrimony, and I have, on certain conditions,
" agreed to affift him; but whatever you may hear, or
" fee, be affur'd that nothing is fo impoffible, as that he
" fhou'd become the hufband of *Donna Marcella.*"——
Oh delightful girl! how I love her for this!

MIN. Yes, Ma'am; and if you'd had patience, I fhou'd have told you that fhe's now here with Don Cæfar, in grave debate how to begin the attack, which muft force you to take fhelter in the arms of a hufband.

OLIV. Ah, no matter how they begin it.—Let them

amufe

amufe themfelves in raifing batteries ; my referv'd fire
fhall tumble them about their ears, in the moment my poor
father is finging his Io's for victory.——But here come
the lovers.——Well, I proteft now, fixteen and fixty is a
very comely fight——'Tis contraft gives effect to every
thing——Lud ! how my father ogles ! I had no idea he
was fuch a fort of man.—I am really afraid he isn't quite
fo good as he fhou'd be.

Enter Don Cæsar *leading* Marcella.

Cæs. H—um—Madam looks very placid ; we fhall
difcompofe her, or I am miftaken. [*apart*] So, Olivia, here's
Donna Marcella come to vifit you—though, as matters
are, that refpect was due from you.

Oliv. I am fenfible of the condefcenfion—My dear
Ma'am, how very good this is. [*taking her hand.*]

Cæs. Yes, you'll think yourfelf wonderfully oblig'd,
when you know all. [*afide.*] Pray, Donna Marcella,
what do you think of thefe apartments ? The furniture
and decorations are my daughter's tafte ; wou'd you
wifh them to remain, or will you give orders to have them
chang'd ?

Marc. Chang'd, undoubtedly ; I can have nobody's
tafte govern my apartments but my own.

Cæs. Ah, that touches—See how fhe looks. [*apart.*]
They fhall receive your orders.——You underftand, I
fuppofe, from this, that every thing is fix'd on between
Donna Marcella and me ?

Oliv. Yes, Sir ; I underftand it perfectly, and it
gives me infinite pleafure.

Cæs. Eh ! pleafure !

Oliv. Entirely, Sir——

Cæs.

Cæs. Tol-de-rol ! Ah that won't do—that won't do.
—You can't hide it.—You are frighten'd out of your wits
at the thoughts of a mother-in-law,—eſpecially a young,
gay, handſome one.

Oliv. Pardon me, Sir ; the thought of a mother-in-
law was indeed diſagreeable ; but her being young and
gay qualifies it.——I hope, Ma'am, you'll give us balls,
and the moſt ſpirited parties——You can't think how ſtupid we have been.—My dear father hates thoſe things—
but I hope now——

Cæs. Hey, hey, hey ! what's the meaning of all this ?
Why, huſſey, don't you know you'll have no apartment
but the garret ?

Oliv. That will benefit my complexion, Sir, by
mending my health. 'Tis charming to ſleep in an elevated
ſituation.

Cæs. Here ! here's an obſtinate perverſe ſlut !

Oliv. Bleſs me, Sir, are you angry that I look for-
wards to your marriage without murmuring ?

Cæs. Yes, I am—yes, I am—you ought to murmur,
and you ought to—to—to——

Oliv. Dear me ! I find love taken up late in life, has
a bad effect on the temper —I wiſh, my dear papa, you
had felt the influence of Donna Marcella's charms ſome-
what ſooner.

Cæs. You do ! you do ! why this muſt be all put on.
—This can't be real.

Oliv. Indeed, indeed it is ; and I proteſt your engagement with this lady has given me more pleaſure than
I have taſted ever ſince you began to teaze me about a huſ-
band. You ſeem'd determin'd to have a marriage in the
family ;

family; and I hope now I fhall live in quiet, with my dear, fweet, young mother-in-law.

CÆS. Oh—oh [*walking about.*] Was there ever——— She doesn't care for a mother-in-law !——Can't frighten her !

OLIV. Sure, my fate is very peculiar; that being pleas'd with your choice, and fubmitting with humble duty to your will, fhou'd be the caufe of offence.

CÆS. Huffey ! I don't want you to be pleas'd with my choice—I don't want you to fubmit with humble duty to my will———Where I do want you to fubmit, you rebel— You are a—you are———But I'll mortify that wayward fpirit yet.   [*Exit Don* CÆSAR *and* MARCELLA.

MIN. Well, really, my mafter is in a piteous paffion —he feems more angry at your liking his marriage, than at your refufing to be married yourfelf.———Wouldn't it have been better, Madam, to have affected difcontent ?

OLIV. To what purpofe ? but to lay myfelf open to frefh folicitations, in order to get rid of the evil I pre- tended to dread ! Blefs us ! nothing can be more eafy than for my father to be gratified, if he were but lucky in the choice of a lover.

MIN. As much as to fay, Madam, that there is———

OLIV. Why, yes, "as much as to fay"—I fee you are refolv'd to have my fecret, Minette, and fo———

Enter SERVANT.

SERV. There is a gentleman at the door, Madam, call'd Don Julio de Meleffina. He waits on you from Don Vincentio.

OLIV. Who ? Don Julio ! it cannot be—art thou fure of his name ?

SERV. The fervant repeated it twice—He is in a fine carriage, and feems to be a nobleman.

OLIV. Conduct him hither.   [*Exeunt Servant.*

I am aftonifh'd; I cannot fee him.—I wou'd not have him know the incognita to be Olivia for worlds !—There is but one way. [*afide.*] Minette, afk no queftions, but do as I order you—Receive Don Julio in my name ; call yourfelf the heirefs of Don Cæfar, and on no account fuffer him to believe that you are any thing elfe.   [*turning from her.*

I am amaz'd and confus'd !——It is impoffible that he can have difcover'd me—Perhaps he comes with offers to my father—then my interview laft night did not give him thofe impreffions I hop'd.——I am jealous of myfelf.— If it is fo, his *incognito* fhall never pardon a paffion for *the daughter of Don Cæfar.*   [*Exit.*

MIN. So ! then, this is fome new lover whom fhe is determined to difguft ; and fancies that making me pafs for her, will compleat it. Perhaps her ladyfhip may be miftaken, though. [*Looking thro' the wing*] Upon my word, a fweet man ! Oh, lud, my heart beats with the very idea of his making love to me, even though he takes me for another—Stay, I think he fha'nt find me here—Standing in the middle of a room gives one's appearance no effect.— I'll enter upon him with an eafy fwim, or an engaging trip, or a—fomething that fhall ftrike—the firft glance is every thing.   [*Exit.*

Enter JULIO, *preceded by Servant, who retires.*

JULIO. Not here ! The ridiculous difpute between Garcia and Vincentio, gives me irrefiftable curiofity——though, if fhe is the character Garcia defcribes, I expect

to be cuff'd for my impertinence——Here fhe comes !——
A pretty, little, fmiling girl, 'faith, for a vixen.

Enter MINETTE, *very affectedly.*

MIN.   Sir, your moft obedient humble fervant.   You
are Don Julio de Meleffina.   I am extremely glad to fee
you, Sir.

JULIO. [*afide.*]   A very courteous reception ! ——You
honour me infinitely, Madam—I muft apologize for waiting on you without a better introduction—Don Vincentio
promis'd to attend me, but a concert call'd him to another
part of the town, at the moment I prepar'd to come hither.

MIN.   A concert——Yes, Sir, he is very fond of
mufic.

JULIO.   He is, Madam :—You, I fuppofe, have a paffion
for that charming fcience ?

MIN.   Oh, yes, I love it mightily.

JULIO. [*Afide.*]   This is lucky !   I think I have heard,
Donna Olivia, that your tafte that way is peculiar ; you
are fond of a——faith I can hardly fpeak it. [*afide*]—of a
——Jew's harp.   [*fmothering a laugh*]

MIN.   A *Jew's harp* !   Mercy !   What do you think a
perfon of my birth and figure, can have fuch fancies as
that ?   No, Sir, I love fiddles, French horns, tabors, and
all the chearful, noify inftruments in the world.

JULIO. [*Afide.*]   Vincentio muft have been mad ; and
I as mad as him to mention it.   Then you are fond of
concerts, Madam ?

MIN.   Doat on 'em !   I wifh he'd offer me a ticket.
[*afide.*

JULIO. [*Afide.*]   Vincentio is clearly wrong.—Now to
prove how far the other was right, in fuppofing her a vixen.

MIN.

MIN. There is a grand public concert, Sir, to be to-morrow. Pray do you go?

JULIO. I believe I fhall have that pleafure, Madam.

MIN. My father, Don Cæfar, won't let me purchafe a ticket: I think it's very hard.

JULIO. Pardon me, I think it's perfectly right.

MIN. Right! what to refufe me a trifling expence, that would procure me a great pleafure?

JULIO. Yes, doubtlefs——The ladies are too fond of pleafure.—I think Don Cæfar is exemplary.

MIN. Lord, Sir, you'd think it very hard if you were me, to be lock'd up all your life, and know nothing of the world but what you cou'd catch through the bars of your balcony.

JULIO. Perhaps I might; but as a man, I am convinc'd 'tis right. Daughters and wives fhould be equally excluded thofe deftructive haunts of diffipation.—Let them keep to their embroidery, nor ever prefume to fhew their faces but at their own fire fides.——This will bring out the Xan-tippe, furely. [*afide.*]

MIN. Well, Sir, I don't know—to be fure, home, as you fay, is the fitteft place for women.—For my part, I cou'd live for ever at home. I am determin'd he fhall have his way—who knows what may happen. [*afide.*

JULIO. [*Afide.*] By all the powers of caprice, Garcia is as wrong as the other!

MIN. I delight in nothing fo much as in fitting by my father, and hearing his tales of old times—and I fancy, when I have a hufband, I fhall be more happy to fit and liften to his ftories of prefent times.

JULIO. Perhaps your hufband, fair lady, might not be inclined

inclined *so* to amufe you.—Men have a thoufand delights that call them abroad ; and probably your chief amufements wou'd be counting the hours of his abfence, and giving a tear to each as it pafs'd.

MIN. Well, he fhou'd never fee 'em, however. I wou'd always fmile when *he* enter'd, and if he found my eyes red, I'd fay I had been weeping over the hiftory of the unfortunate damfel, whofe true love hung himfelf at fea, and appear'd to her afterwards in a wet jacket.—— Sure this will do. [*afide.*]

JULIO. I am every moment more aftonifh'd ! Pray, Madam, permit me a queftion—Are you really—yet I cannot doubt it—are you really Donna Olivia, the daughter of Don Cæfar, to whom Don Garcia and Don Vincentio, had lately the honour of paying their addreffes ?

MIN. Am I Donna Olivia ! ha, ha, ha ! what a queftion ! . Pray, Sir is this my father's houfe ?—are you Don Julio ?

JULIO. I beg your pardon ; but, to confefs, I had heard you defcrib'd as a lady who had not quite fo much fweetnefs, and——

MIN. Oh, what you had heard that I was a termagant, I fuppofe——'Tis all flander, Sir—There is not in Madrid, though I fay it, a fweeter temper than my own ; and though I have refus'd a good many lovers, yet if one was to offer himfelf, that I cou'd like——

JULIO. You wou'd take pity, and reward his paffion. Lovely Donna Olivia, how charming is this franknefs ! ——'tis a little odd, though ! [*afide.*]

MIN. Why, I believe, I fhou'd take pity, for it always feem'd to me to be very hard-hearted to be cruel to

2

a lover that one likes, becaufe in that cafe one fhou'd——
a——You know, Sir, the fooner the affair is over, the
better for both parties.

JULIO. What the deuce does fhe mean?—Is this Garcia's four fruit?

CÆSAR, *without.*

Olivia!—Olivia!

MIN. Blefs me, I hear my father! Now, Sir, I have
a particular fancy that you fhou'd not tell him, in this firft
vifit, your defign.

JULIO. Madam! my defign!

MIN. Yes, that you will not fpeak out, 'till we have·
had a little further converfation, which I'll take care to
give you an opportunity for very foon.——He'll be here
in a moment—Now, pray Don Julio, go—If he fhou'd
meet you, and afk who you are, you can fay that you
are—you may fay that you came on a vifit to my maid,
you know.

JULIO. I thank you, Madam—[*aloud.*]—for my dif-
miffion—[*afide.*] I never was in fuch peril in my life.——
I believe fhe has a licenfe in her pocket, a prieft in her
clofet, and the ceremony by heart. [*Exit.*

END OF THE FOURTH ACT.

F ACT

ACT V. SCENE I.

DON CARLOS'S.

Carlos discover'd writing.

Carlos, [*tearing paper, and rising.*]

IT is in vain ! Language cannot furnish me with terms
to soften to Victoria the horrid transaction. Cou'd she
ee. the compunctions of my soul, her gentle heart wou'd
pity me——But what then ? *She's ruin'd !* My children
are undone ! Oh ! the artifices of one base woman, and
my villainy to another most amiable one, has made me
unfit to live.—I am a wretch who ought to be blotted from
society.

Enter PEDRO *hastily.*

PED. Sir, Sir.

CAR. Well !

PED. Sir, I have just met Don Florio ; he ask'd if
my mistress was at home, so I guesses he is going to our
house, and so I run to let you know—for I loves to keep
my promises, though I am deadly afraid of some mischief.

CAR. You have done well.—Go home, and wait for me
at the door, and admit me without noise. [*Exit Pedro.*] At
least then, I shall have the pleasure of revenge ; I'll
punish that harlot by sacrificing her paramour in her
arms—and then——Oh ! [*Exit.*

Scene

Scene changes to DONNA LAURA'S.

Enter LAURA *with precipitation, followed by* VICTORIA.

LAU. 'Tis his carriage!—How fuccefsful was my letter! This, my Florio, is a moſt important moment.

VICT. It is indeed ; and I will leave you to make
every advantage of it. If I am prefent, I muſt witnefs
condefcenſions from you, that I ſhall not be able to bear,
though I know them to be but affected.——Now, Gaſper,
play thy part well, and fave Victoria! [*aſide.*]

[*Exit.*

LAU. This tender jealouſy is dear to me!—Keep in
the faloon. Here comes the dotard.

Enter GASPER, *dreſſed as an old Beau, two Servants follow
him, and take off a rich cloak.*

GASP. Take my cloak ; and, d'ye hear, Ricardo, go
home and bring the eider-down cuſhions for the coach,
and tell the fellow not to hurry me *poſt* through the
ſtreets of Madrid. I have been jolted from ſide to ſide,
like a pippin in a mill ſtream.—Drive a man of my rank,
as he wou'd a city vintner and his fat wife, going to a
bull fight!——Hah, there ſhe is! [*looking through a glaſs,
fuſpended by a red ribbon.*]——there ſhe is! Charming
Donna Laura, let me thus at the ſhrine of your beauty—
[*makes an effort to kneel, and falls on his face ; Laura aſ-
ſiſts him to rife.*] Fye, fye, thoſe new ſhoes!—they have
made me ſkate all day, like a Dutchman on a canal, and
now—Well, you fee how profound my adoration is, Madam.—Common lovers kneel ; *I* was proſtrate.

LAU. You do me infinite honour.——Difguſtful
wretch!

F 2

GASP.

GASP. But how cou'd you be fo barbarous, to leave me at Valencia, without granting me one interview nearer than your balcony ?

LAU. I will be ingenuous—it was female artifice. I knew you wou'd follow me ; and how cou'd I refift the *triumph* of fhewing that I led in my chains the illuftrious Don Sancho ?

GASP. Oh you dear charming——But ftay [*fearching his pockets.*]——Blefs me, what a a carelefs fellow I am ! I had a cafket, with fome diamonds in it—a necklace, and a few trifles, which I meant to have had the honour of placing on your toilette——Left it at home——Oh, my giddy pate !

LAU. You are always elegant, Don Sancho. I'll fend my fervant.——Pedro ! [*calling.*]

GASP. No, no, to-morrow. It will be an excufe for me to come to morrow.——I fhall often want excufes.

LAU. *My wifhes* fhall always be your excufe, but to-morrow be it then. You are thinner than you were, Don Sancho.—I proteft, now I obferve you, you are much alter'd.

GASP. Aye, Madam——Fretting. Your abfence threw me into a fever, and that deftroy'd my bloom :—— You fee I look almoft a middle-aged man, now.

LAU. No, really ; far from it, I affure you.——The fop is as wrinkled as a baboon. [*afide.*]

GASP. Then, jealoufy, *that* gave me a jaundice. My niece's hufband, I hear, Don Carlos, has been my happy rival—Oh, my blade will hardly keep in its fcabbard, when I think of him.

LAU. Think no more of him—He has been long ba-
niſh'd

nifh'd my thoughts, be affured. I wonder you gave your niece to him, with fuch a fortune.

GASP. Gave! She gave herfelf; and as to fortune, fhe had not a piftole from me.

LAU. 'Twas indeed unneceffary, with fo fine an eftate as fhe had in Leon.

GASP. My niece an eftate in Leon! Not enough to give fhelter to a field moufe; and if he has told you fo, he is a braggart.

LAU. Told me fo——I have the writings; he has made over the lands to me.

GASP. Made over the lands to you——Oh a deceiver! I begin to fufpect a plot. Pray let me fee this extraordinary deed. [*She runs to a cabinet.*] A plot, I'll be fworn.

LAU. Here is the deed which made that eftate mine forever. No, Sir, I will intruft it in no hand but my own—Yet look over me, and read the defcription of the lands.

GASP. [*Reading through his glafs.*] H—m—m— : "In the vicinage of Rofalva, bounded on the weft by the river —h—m—m, on the eaft by the foreft——" Oh, an artful dog! I need read no further; I fee how the thing is.

LAU. How, Sir!——but hold——Stay a moment—I am breathlefs with fear.

GASP. Nay, Madam, don't be afraid! 'Tis my eftate—that's all—the very caftle where I was born, and which I never did, nor ever will beftow on any Don in the two Caftiles. Diffembling rogue! Bribe you with a fictitious title to my eftate, ha, ha, ha!

LAU. [*Afide.*] Curfes follow him! The villain I em-

ploy'd

ploy'd, muſt have been *his* creature—His reluctance all
art—and, whilſt I believ'd myſelf undoing him, was
duped myſelf!

GASP. Cou'd you ſuppoſe I'd give Carlos ſuch an
eſtate for running away with my niece ? No, no, the
vineyards, and the corn-fields, and the woods of Roſalva,
are not for him.—I've ſomebody elſe in my eye—in my
eye, obſerve me—to give thoſe to ;---can't you gueſs who
it is ?

LAU. No, indeed !——He gives me a glimmering
that ſaves me from deſpair. [*aſide.*]

GASP. I won't tell you, unleſs you'll bribe me.—I
won't indeed——[*kiſſes her cheek.*] There, now I'll tell
you——They are all for you.——Yes, this eſtate, to
which you have taken ſuch a fancy, ſhall be yours.—*I'll*
give you the deeds, if you'll promiſe to love me, you
little, cruel thing!

LAU. Can you be ſerious ?

GASP. I'll ſign and ſeal to-morrow.

LAU. Noble Don Sancho! Thus then I annihilate the
proof of his perfidy and my weakneſs. Thus I tear to
atoms his deteſted name ; and as I tread on theſe, ſo wou'd
I on his heart.

Enter VICTORIA.

VICT. My children then are ſav'd! [*in tranſport.*]

LAU. [*Apart.*] Oh, Florio, 'tis as thou ſaid'ſt—Carlos
was a villain, and deceiv'd me.——Why this ſtrange air ?
Ah, I ſee the cauſe—You think me ruin'd, and will aban-
don me.—Yes, I ſee it in thy averted face ; thou dar'ſt
not meet my eyes.—If I misjudge thee, ſpeak !

VICT. Laura, I cannot ſpeak.——You little gueſs the
emotions of my heart.——Heav'n knows, I pity you!

LAU.

LAU. Pity! Oh, villain! and has thy love already fnatch'd the form of pity? Bafe, deceitful——

CARLOS *without*.

CAR. Stand off, loofe your weak hold; I'm come for vengeance!

Enter CARLOS.

Where is this youth? Where is the blooming rival, for whom I have been betray'd? Hold me not, bafe woman! In vain the ftripling flies me; for, by Heav'n, my fword fhall in his bofom write its mafter's wrongs!

VICTORIA *firft goes towards the flat, then returns, takes off her hat, and drops on one knee.*

VICT. Strike, ftrike it here! Plunge it deep into that bofom already wounded by a thoufand ftabs, keener and more painful than your fword can give.—Here lives all the gnawing anguifh of love betray'd; here live the pangs of difappointed hopes, hopes fanctified by holieft vows, which have been written in the book of Heav'n.——Hah! he finks.——[*She flies to him.*]—Oh! my Carlos! My belov'd! my hufband! forgive my too fevere reproaches; thou art dear, yet dear as ever, to Victoria's heart!

CAR. [*Recovering.*] Oh, you know not what you do—you know not what you are.—Oh, Victoria, thou art a beggar!

VICT. No, we are rich, we are happy! See there, the fragments of that fatal deed, which had I not recover'd, we had been indeed *undone*; yet ftill not *wretched*, cou'd my Carlos think fo!

CAR. The fragments of the deed! the deed which that bafe woman——

VICT. Speak not fo harfhly.——To you, Madam, I fear, I feem reprehenfible; yet when you confider my duties as wife and mother, you will forgive me.—Be not afraid of poverty—a woman has deceiv'd, but fhe will not defert you!

F 4 LAU.

Lau. Is this real ? Can I be awake ?

Vict. Oh, may'ft thou indeed awake to virtue !——
You have talents that might grace the higheft of our fex ;
be no longer unjuft to fuch precious gifts, by burying
them in difhonour.——Virtue is our firft, moft awful duty ; bow, Laura ! bow before her throne, and mourn in
ceafelefs tears, that ever you forgot her heav'nly precepts !

Lau. So, by a fmooth fpeech about virtue, you think
to cover the injuries I fuftain. Vile, infinuating monfter !
—but thou know'ft me not.—Revenge is fweeter to my
heart than love ; and if there is a law in Spain to gratify
that paffion, your *virtue* fhall have another field for exer-
cife. [*Exit.*

Gasp. No, no ; you'll find no help in the law,
charmer ! However, the long robes are rich—get amongft
them ; their gravities may adminifter to your avarice,
though not to your revenge.

Car. [*Turning towards Victoria.*] My hated rival, and
my charming wife ! How many fweet myfteries have you
to unfold !——Oh, Victoria ! my foul thanks thee, but I
dare not yet fay I love thee, 'till ten thoufand acts of
watchful tendernefs, have prov'd how deep the fentiment's
engrav'd.

Vict. Can it be true that I have been unhappy ?——
But the myfteries, my Carlos, are already explain'd to
you—Gafper's refemblance to my uncle——

Gasp. Yes, Sir, I was always apt at refemblances—
In our plays at home, I am always Queen Cleopatra—
You know fhe was but a gypfey Queen, and I hits her off
to a nicety.

Car. Come, my Victoria——Oh, there is a painful
pleafure in my bofom—To gaze on thee, to liften to, and
love thee, feems like the blifs of angels cheering whifpers
to repentant finners ! [*Exeunt Carlos and Victoria.*
Gasp.

GASP. Lord help 'em ! how eafily the women are taken in !——Here's a wild rogue has plagu'd her heart thefe two years, and a whip fyllabub about angels and whifpers clears fcores.——'Tis pity but they were a little——tho', now I think on't, the number of thefe *gentle* fair ones is fo very fmall, that if it was leffen'd, the two fexes might be confounded together, and the whole world be fuppos'd of the mafculine gender.   [*Exit.*

SCENE, THE PRADO.

Enter MINETTE.

MIN. Ah, here comes the man at laft, after I have been fauntering in fight of his lodgings thefe two hours.—— Now, if my fcheme takes, what a happy perfon I fhall be ! and fure, as I was Donna Olivia to-day, to pleafe my lady, I may be Donna Olivia to night, to pleafe myfelf. I'll addrefs him as the maid of a lady who has taken a fancy to him, then convey him to our houfe—then retire, and then come in again, and with a vaft deal of confufion, confefs I fent my maid for him. If he fhould diflike my *forward-nefs*, the cenfure will fall on my lady ; if he fhould be pleas'd with my *perfon*, the advantage will be mine. But perhaps he's come here on fome wicked frolic or other.— I'll watch him at a diftance before I fpeak.   [*Exit.*

Enter JULIO.

JULIO. Not here, 'faith ; though fhe gave me laft night but a faint refufal, and I had a right, by all the rules of gallantry, to conftrue that into an affent.——Then fhe's a jilt—Hang her, I feel I am uneafy—The firft wo-man that ever gave me pain.——I am afham'd to perceive that this fpot has attractions for me, only becaufe it was here I convers'd with her. 'Twas here the little fyren,

con-

conscious of her charms, unveil'd her fascinating face.——
'Twas here——

Enter GARCIA *and* VINCENTIO.

GARC.　'*Twas here* that Julio, leaving champaïgne
untasted, and songs of gallantry unsung, came to talk to
the whistling branches.

VIN.　'*Twas here* that Julio, flying from the young and
gay, was found in doleful meditation——[*altering his
tone.*]—on a wench, for a hundred ducats !

GARC.　Who is she ?

JULIO.　Not Donna Olivia, Gentlemen ; not Donna
Olivia.

GARC.　We have been seeking you, to ask the event
of your visit to her.

JULIO.　The event has prov'd that *you* have been most
grosly dup'd.

VIN.　I knew that—Ha, ha, ha !

JULIO.　And you likewise, *I* know that—Ha, ha ha !
——The fair lady, so far from being a vixen, is the very
essence of gentleness.　To me, so much sweetness in a
wife, wou'd be downright maukish—I like the little acer-
bities which flow from quick spirits, and a consciousness of
power.—One may as well marry a looking-glass as a woman who constantly reflects back one's own sentiments,
and one's own whims.

VIN.　Well, but she's fond of a Jew's harp.

JULIO.　Detests it ; she would be as fond of *a Jew.*

GARC.　Pho, pho, this is a game at cross purposes ;—
Let us all go to Don Cæsar's together, and compare opi-
nions on the spot.

JULIO.　I'll go most willingly—but it will be only to
cover you both with confusion, for being the two men in
Spain most easily impos'd on. [*All going.*]

Enter

Enter MINETTE.

MIN. Gentlemen, my lady has fent me for one of you, pray which of you is it?

JULIO. [*Returning.*] Me, without doubt, child.

VIN. I don't know that.

GARC. Look at me, my dear, don't you think I am the man?

MIN. Let me fee—a good air, and well made, you are the man for a dancer.—[*to Garcia*] Well drefs'd, and nicely put out of hands—you are the man for a bandbox. [*to Vincentio*] Handfome and bold—you are the man for my lady. [*to Julio*]

JULIO. My dear little Iris, here's all the gold in my pocket.—Gentlemen, I wifh you a good night—I am your very obedient, humble—[*ftalking by them with his arm round Minette.*]

GARC. Pho, prithee, don't be a fool. Are we not going to Donna Olivia?

JULIO. Donna Olivia muft wait, my dear boy; we can decide about her to-morrow. Come along, my little dove of Venus! [*Exit.*

GARC. What a rafh fellow it is! ten to one but this is fome common bufinefs, and he'll be robb'd and murder'd—they take him for a ftranger.

VIN. Let's follow, and fee where fhe leads him.

GARC. That's hardly fair, however, as I think there's danger, we will follow. [*Exit.*

SCENE, DON CÆSAR'S

Enter OLIVIA *and* SERVANT.

OLIV. Bring me my veil and follow me to the Prado.
[*Exit Servant.*
Julio

Julio will certainly be there—he has too much breeding not to tranſlate my poſitive denial into aſſent—at leaſt I muſt convince myſelf. If I ſee him compleatly vanquiſh'd, I can, by the moſt *unlucky chance in the world*, drop a card with my name, and then all the reſt follows in courſe,   [*Exit.*

Enter MINETTE *and* JULIO.

MIN. There, Sir, pleaſe to ſit down, 'till my lady is ready to wait on you—ſhe won't be long. . . . . I'm ſure ſhe's out, and I may do great things before ſhe returns. [*aſide*
                                                                        [*Exit.*

JULIO. Through fifty back lanes, a long garden, and a narrow ſtair-caſe, into a ſuperb apartment—all that's in the regular way ; as the Spaniſh women manage it, one intrigue is too much like another, whilſt the ſprightly dames of Paris have the art of giving the ſame intrigue every day a new air. Now, preſently, in comes a ſtately dame with a veil on ; ſhe tells me, ſhe fears I have but a ſlight opinion of her virtue ; I make her an anſwer about her beauty, and, after a dozen or two entreaties and de-nials, off comes her veil. A fat matron, perhaps of for-ty—I ſwear ſhe's a Hebe—ſhe thinks me very obliging, and I find her very grateful ; and this is the epitome of half the amours in Madrid. If it was not now and then for the little lively fillip of a jealous huſband or brother, which obliges one to leap from a window, or crawl, like a cat, along the gutters, there would be no bearing the *ennui.* Ah ! ah ! but this promiſes novelty ; [*looking through the wing*] a young girl and an old man—wife or daughter ? They are coming this way. My lovely incog-nita, by all that's propitious ! Why did not ſome kind
                                                                        ſpirit

fpirit whifper to me my happinefs? but hold—fhe can't
mean to treat the old gentleman with a fight of me.

[goes behind the fopha.

Enter CÆSAR *and* OLIVIA.

CÆS.   No, no, Madam, no going out—give me your
veil ; that will be ufelefs 'till you put it on for life.   There,
madam, this is your *apartment*, your *houfe*, your *garden*, your *affembly*, 'till you go to your convent.   Why,
how impudent you are, to look thus unconcern'd !—Can
hardly forbear laughing in my face !—Very well—very
well !   *[Exit, double locking the door.*

OLIV.   Ha, ha, ha! I'll be even with you, my dear
father, if you treble lock it.   I'll ftay here two days,
without once afking for my liberty, and you'll come the
third, with tears in your eyes, to take me out.—He has
forgot that door leading to the garden—but I vow I'll
ftay, *[fitting down]* I can make the time pafs pleafantly
enough.

JULIO.   I hope fo.   *[looking over the back of the fopha.*

OLIV.   Heav'n and earth !

JULIO.   My dear creature, why are you fo alarmed ;
am I here before you expected me ?   *[coming round.*

OLIV.   Expected you !

JULIO.   Oh, this pretty furprize ! Come, let us fit
down, I think your father was very obliging to lock us in
together.

OLIV.   Sir, Sir ! my father !   *[calling at the door.*

CÆS.   *[without]* Aye, 'tis all in vain—I won't come
near you.   There you are, and there you may ftay.—I
fhan't return, make as much noife as you will.

JULIO.   Why are you not afham'd that your father
has fo much more confideration for your gueft than you
have ?

OLIV.

OLIV. My gueſt! how is it poſſible he can have diſ-
cover'd me!   [aſide.

JULIO. Pho, this is carrying the thing further than
you need—if there was a third perſon here, it might be
prudent.

OLIV. Why, this aſſurance, Don Julio, is really—

JULIO. The thing in the world you are moſt ready to
pardon.

OLIV. Upon my word I don't know how to treat
you.

JULIO. Conſult your heart!

OLIV. I ſhall conſult my honour.

JULIO. Honour is a pretty thing to play with, but
when ſpoken with that very grave face, after having ſent
your maid to bring me here, is really more than I expected. I ſhall be in an ill humour preſently—I won't
ſtay if you treat me thus.

OLIV. Well, this is ſuperior to every thing! I have
heard that men will ſlander women privately to each
other, 'tis their common amuſement, but to do it to
one's face!—and you really pretend that I ſent for you?

JULIO. Ha, ha, ha! Well, if it obliges you, I will
pretend that you did not ſend for me; that your maid did
not conduct me hither, nay, that I have not now the ſu-
preme happineſs——   [catching her in his arms.

Enter MINETTE, ſcreams and runs out.

JULIO. Donna Olivia de Zuniga! how the devil
came ſhe here?

OLIV. [Aſide] That's lucky! Olivia, my dear friend,
why do you run away? Keep the character, I charge
you. [apart to Minette] Be ſtill Olivia!

                                                    MIN.

MIN. Oh! dear madam! I was——I was so frighten'd when I saw that gentleman.

OLIV. Oh, my dear, it's the merriest pretty kind of. gentleman in the world; he pretends that I sent my maid for him into the streets, ha, ha!

JULIO. That's. right, always tell a thing yourself, which you wou'd not have believ'd.

MIN. It is the readiest excuse for being found in a lady's apartment, however. Now will I swear I know nothing of. the matter. [aside.

OLIV. Now, I think it a horrid poor excuse, he has certainly not had occasion to invent reasons for such impertinencies often. Tell me that he has made love to you to day. [apart.

MIN. I fancy that he *has* had occasion to excuse impertinencies often;——his impertinence to me to day——

JULIO. To you, madam?

MIN. Making love to me, my dear, all the morning ——could hardly get him away he was so desirous to speak to my father. Nay, Sir, I don't care for your impatience.

JULIO. [*Aside*] Now wou'd I give a thousand pistoles if she were a man!

OLIV. Nay, then, this accidental meeting is fortunate—pray, Don Julio, don't let my presence prevent your saying what you think proper to my friend—shall I leave you together?

JULIO. [*Apart*] To contradict a lady on such an assertion wou'd be too gross; but, upon my honour, Donna Olivia is the last woman upon earth who cou'd inspire

me

me with a tender idea. Find an excuse to send her away, my angel, I entreat you. I have a thousand things to say, and the moments are too precious to be given to her.

OLIV. I think so too, but one can't be rude, you know. Come, my dear, sit down, [*seating herself*] have you brought your work?

JULIO. The devil! what can she mean? [*pushing himself between Minette and the sopha*] Donna Olivia, I am sorry to inform you that my physician has just been sent for to your father, Don Cæsar.—The poor gentleman was seized with a vertigo.

OLIV. Vertigoes! Oh, he has 'em frequently you know. [*to Minette.*]

MIN. Yes, and they always keep me from his sight.

JULIO. Did ever one women prevent another from leaving her at such a moment before? I really, madam, cannot comprehend——

CÆSAR *without.*

It is impossible—impossible, gentlemen? Don Julio cannot be here.

JULIO. Hah, who's that?

Enter CÆSAR, GARCIA, *and* VINCENTIO.

GARC. There! did we not tell you so? we saw him enter the garden.

CÆS. What can be the meaning of all this? A man in my daughter's apartment! [*attempting to draw.*

GARC. Hold, Sir! Don Julio is of the first rank in Spain, and will unquestionably be able to satisfy your honour, without troubling your sword.—We have done mischief, Vincentio! [*apart.*

JULIO.

JULIO. [*to Olivia*] They have been curſedly impertinent! but I'll bring you off, never fear, by pretending a paſſion for your buſy friend, there.

CÆS. Satisfy me then in a moment; ſpeak, one of you.

JULIO. I came here, Sir, by the mereſt accident.— The garden door was open, curioſity led me to this apartment.—You came in a moment after, and very civilly lock'd me in with your daughter.

CÆS. Lock'd you in! why then, did you not, like a man of honour, cry out?

JULIO. The lady cried out, Sir, and you told her you would not return; but when Donna Olivia de Zuniga entered, for whom I have conceived a moſt violent paſſion——

CÆS. A paſſion for her! Oh, let me hear no more on't.—A paſſion for her! You may as well entertain a paſſion for the untameable hyæna.

GARC. There, Vincentio, what think you now? Xantippe or not!

VIN. I am afraid I muſt give up that—but pray ſupport me as to this point, Don Cæſar; is not the lady fond of a Jew's harp?

CÆS. Fond! She's fond of nothing, but playing the vixen; there is not ſuch a fury upon earth.

JULIO. Theſe are odd liberties, with a perſon who does not belong to him.

CÆS. I'll play the hypocrite for her no more; the world ſhall know her true charaſter, they ſhall know—— but aſk her maid there.

JULIO. Her maid!

MIN. Why, yes, Sir, to ſay truth, I am but Donna Olivia's maid, after all.

G   OLIV.

OLIV. [*Apart*] Dear Minette! fpeak for me, or I am now ruin'd.

MIN. I will, ma'am.—I muft confefs, Sir, [*going up to Julio*] there never was fo bitter a temper'd creature, as my lady is. I have borne her humours for two years; I have feen her by night and by day. [*Olivia pulls her fleeve, impatiently*] I will, I will! [*to Olivia*] and this I am fure, that if you marry her, you'll rue the day every hour the firft month, and hang yourfelf the next. There, madam, I have done it roundly now.

OLIV. I am undone.—I am caught in my own fnare.
[*afide.*

CÆS. After this true character of my daughter, I fuppofe, Signor, we fhall hear no more of your paffion; fo let us go down, and leave madam to begin her penance.

JULIO. My ideas are totally confus'd.—You Donna Olivia de Zuniga, and the perfon I thought you, her maid! fomething too flattering darts acrofs my mind.

CÆS. If you have taken a fancy to her maid, I have nothing farther to fay, but as to that violent creature.——

JULIO. Oh, do not prophane her.—Where is that fpirit which you tell me of? Is it that which fpeaks in modeft, confcious blufhes on her checks? Is it that which bends her lovely eyes to earth?

CÆS. Ay, fhe's only bending 'em to earth, confidering how to afflict me with fome new obftinacy—fhe'll break out like a tygrefs in a moment.

JULIO. It cannot be—*are* you, charming woman! fuch a creature?

OLIV. Yes, to all mankind—but one. [*looking down.*

JULIO. But one! Oh, might that excepted one, be me!

OLIV

OLIV. Wou'd you not fear to truſt your fate with her, you have cauſe to think ſo hateful?

JULIO. No, I'd bleſs the hour that bound my fate to her's—permit me, Sir, to pay my vows to this fair vixen.

CÆS. What are you ſuch a bold man as that? Pho, but if you are, 'twill be only loſt time—ſhe'll contrive ſome way or other, to return your vows upon your hands.

OLIV. If they have your authority, Sir, I will return them—only with my own.

CÆS. What's that! what did ſhe ſay? my head is giddy with ſurprize.

JULIO. And mine with rapture. [catching her hand.

CÆS. Don't make a fool of me, Olivia.—Wil't marry him?

OLIV. When you command me, Sir.

CÆS. My dear Don Julio, thou art my guardian angel—ſhall I have a ſon-in-law at laſt? Garcia, Vincentio, cou'd you have thought it?

GARC. No, Sir, if we had, we ſhould have ſav'd that lady much trouble; 'tis pretty clear now, *why* ſhe was a vixen.

VIN. Yes, yes, 'tis clear enough, and I beg your pardon, madam, for the ſhare of trouble *I* gave you—but pray have the goodneſs to tell me ſincerely, what do you think of a craſh?

OLIV. I love muſic, Don Vincentio, I admire your ſkill, and whenever you'll give me a concert, I ſhall be oblig'd.

VIN. You cou'd not have pleas'd me ſo well, if you had married me.

Enter CARLOS *and* VICTORIA.

OLIV. Hah, here comes Victoria and her Carlos.

My

My friend, you are happy—'tis in your eyes, I need not aſk the event.

CÆS. What is this Don Carlos, whom Victoria gave us for a couſin ? Sir, you come in happy hour !

CAR. I do indeed, for I am moſt happy.

JULIO. My dear Carlos, what has new made thee thus, ſince morning ?

CAR. A wife ! Marry, Julio, marry !

JULIO. What ! this advice from *you* ?

CAR. Yes; and when you have married an angel, when that angel has done for you ſuch things, as makes your gratitude almoſt equal to your love, you may then gueſs ſomething of what I feel, in calling *this* angel mine.

OLIV. Now, I truſt, Don Julio, after all this, that if I ſhould do you the honour of my hand, you'll treat me cruelly, be a very bad man, that I, like my exemplary couſin——

VICT. Hold, Olivia ! it is not neceſſary that a huſ-band ſhould be *faulty*, to make a wife's character *exem-plary*.—Should he be tenderly watchful of your happi-neſs, your gratitude will give a thouſand graces to your conduct ; whilſt the purity of your manners,—and the nice honour of your life, will gain you the approbation of thoſe, whoſe praiſe is fame.

OLIV. Pretty and matronly ! thank you, my dear. We have each ſtruck a bold ſtroke to-day ;—your's has been to reclaim a huſband, mine to get one ; but the moſt important is yet to be obtain'd. ——The approbation of our judges.

That meed with-held our labours have been vain ;
Pointleſs *my* jeſts, and doubly keen your pain ;
Might we their plaudits, and their praiſe provoke,
Our *bell* ſhould then be term'd, a *happy* ſtroke.

T H E   E N D.

EPILOGUE.

BY A GENTLEMAN.

YOUR fervant, friends, from Spain, you fee, I'm come,
    A peace abroad,—but is it peace at home ?
The fword is fheath'd, our heroes all are quiet,
A *gentle* woman I, and hate a riot.
To pick a lover from a croud of beaus,
A lady-ftroke, though bold, you'll fcarce oppofe.
To night you've had a trial of our fkill
In curing lethargy, that growing ill ;
That lifelefs inattention and neglect,
Which fome deferve, fome fear, and fome expect ;
Say, do you like our fcheme ? methinks I hear
A reverend fire, beyond his fixtieth year,
In grumbling accents, faying, " Stuff, fad ftuff !
" Now there's a peace, you may have men enough :—
" They want a leg, perhaps, what's that to you ?
" They're *Frenchmen only*, who make ufe of *two*.
" Then ftay your whining, let your bold ftrokes ceafe,
" Each wound in war, is a bold ftroke for peace."
    How weak your wit, ye lords of the creation,
When fet to find a woman's inclination ;
Her heart, though ice, the virgin fair and young,
Without an ear, with double fhare of tongue ;
Let the fond youth fhe likes, but once appear,
His dulcet voice with rapture fhe can hear ;

                                  If

If she cou'd frown, by smiles her pride's disarm'd;
She *has* a heart, when *love* that heart has warm'd;
No tones discordant now, not even nay,   ⎫
While sighs to sighs responsive seem to say,   ⎬
In accents sweet,——" love, honour and obey."   ⎭

    Dear liberty, farewell! from babe to wife,
I've led a pretty, happy, checquer'd life;
I'll tell you how, the tale's not very long,
But, if you please, I'll give it you in song.

A I R.

When I was a little baby,
Plump and round as may be,
    For a lullaby
    I'd fret and cry,
When I was a little baby.

But at six years old, how froward,
Naughty girl, untoward,
    To dress my doll,
    And prate like poll,
A naughty girl untoward.

At twelve, what a blooming flower!
Around me every hour
    Butterflies gay,
    To sip and play,
Flew round this blooming flower.

At sweet sixteen, so pretty,
All I said was witty;
    A charming lass,
    So said my glass,
At dear sixteen so pretty.

Love's

Love's dart no more to parry,
At twenty-two to marry,
          To one dear youth
          I plight my truth,
And that's the youth I'll marry.

With him I'll toy and play fo,
He'll wonder why I ftay fo ;
          But your applaufe
          Muft crown my caufe,
So clap your hands and fay fo.

F I N I S.

Of the PUBLISHER may be had,

By the fame AUTHOR,

The BELLE's STRATAGEM, a Comedy.

The RUN .WAY, a Comedy.

WHICH IS THE MAN ? a Comedy.

ALBINA, a Tragedy.

WHO's THE DUPE ? a Farce.

THE MAID OF ARRAGON, a Poem.

In the Prefs, and fpeedily will be publifhed,

MRS. COWLEY's laft New COMEDY, call'd,

MORE WAYS THAN ONE.